Say Something Nice

ILHY

SAY SOMETHING NICE

Published by:
Ilhy Gómez Del Campo Rojas
http://bit.ly/ilhysaysomethingnice

Published in the United States of America

ISBN: 9781670066138

For Sammy,

You glorious thing, you.

PART ONE

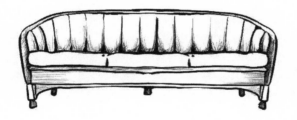

Prologue:

Waking Up the Morning After

I had a terrible dream last night, although when I woke up I learned it was not a dream at all and was, in fact, a very real event that occurred the day before.

My best friend had been murdered.

I ask that you not give me any sympathy or pity since we weren't close at all. Though if she were alive she'd say otherwise. If I knew her better, I could say with absolute certainty that she was the kindest and most peculiar person I have ever had the pleasure of meeting. The way she welcomed strangers into her life was practically poetic; she wanted nothing more than to spread love and respect in every way imaginable. She was an angel our planet didn't deserve, yet we appreciated her as best we could.

However, I didn't know her suitably enough to say any of this with confidence, but there was a time when I thought I could. If there's something I learned from last night, it's that not all with wide smiles and loud laughs are truly content. Nevertheless, we wish they were.

I woke up from a terrible dream this morning, only to find out I hadn't been dreaming at all.

So I went back to sleep.

Chapter One:

We Meet Again Under Better Circumstances

I lowered my window and took in the crisp autumn air in order to ignore the other person inside the car with me. "Darling, we really should get a new car; the new ones have air conditioners! That way you won't have to stick your head out the window all the time," my wife said. I rolled my eyes and stuck my head out farther, hoping I'd somehow slither out and get crushed by the cars behind us.

"Perhaps later," I muttered, not wanting the conversation to continue.

"Well then. Should I change for the party, darling?" I cringed at the pet name she had given me.

"I'm terribly sorry, Helen, truly I am, but you are not allowed to come," I said.

"Wh—well why not? It's been ages since I've been to a party, and I'd like to meet Ruth!" Helen argued, her voice rising. I could only sigh in response.

"I'm sorry, Helen. Maybe next time," I lied.

"Then what am I to do while you're gone?" she whined.

I looked out the window and grinned at the passing trees. *There is a wonderful opera house near the place we're staying, and I heard there would be a show tonight. You could go on my behalf, tell me how it went.* The words ached at the tip of my tongue, but I restrained myself, knowing she would only whine and complain.

"I suppose I'll find something. Perhaps I'll read." She sighed. I forced a pitiful smile and took her hand.

"I wish you could come with me, Helen; really, I do. I would love nothing more than to proudly introduce you to each guest as my wife and watch as all the men give jealous looks. However, Ruth's parties are very small and restricted, and she has given strict directions for me to come alone." I kissed her cheek and slid my hand away, returning my gaze to the world outside. "Besides, I'm certain it'll be a bore."

She smiled and looked out at the road ahead, her chin higher than it was before.

Ruth lived in a marble mansion; the entrance was long and wide, surrounded by an odd combination of shrubs and flowers. "My! Walter, is it really you?" I heard someone shout. My heart skipped a beat as I looked up and saw Ruth standing by the door, wearing a long yellow gown. Her red hair was draped around her shoulders, wrapping around a large silver necklace impossible to ignore. She radiated positivity and warmth, now more than usual.

"Ruth! It has been far too long since I've seen you. I don't know how I've survived this long without one of your infamous hugs!" I exclaimed, almost giggling at the sight of her open arms.

She raced over and squeezed me, practically engulfing me in love. "Oh, Walter, I missed you so much. You always know exactly how to make me blush." She cupped my head in her hands, kissing my forehead. "Where's your wife? I thought you'd introduce me to her today."

I shrugged. "Helen isn't big on parties. She said she was exhausted and didn't want to ruin the event with her sour mood."

Ruth laughed. "Well, maybe next time she'll join us. Now come inside, I want you to meet everyone. Which, before we enter, are you finally singing?"

"I'm afraid not. It still feels like a childish dream."

Ruth took my hand, making my knees feel weak. "Walter, you have the voice of an angel. Please try, for me. Let others be blessed with your magnificent singing; I want you to fill opera houses with your powerful voice." I raised her hand to my lips and kissed it, smiling. It had been far too long since I had last genuinely smiled at someone.

"As long as you're in the front row, dead center. Only then will I give the performance of a lifetime."

Ruth took my hands and dragged me into her home, laughing to herself as I stumbled into her immense home.

A large chandelier swung from a dome ceiling, encircled by paintings of angels and night skies. A large, marble stairway led to a hallway with six bedrooms and three bathrooms; a door next to the staircase led to the ballroom, and finally, the entrance to the dining room stood in front of the stairs, displaying a beautifully decorated table. The whole house was far too refined for someone as chaotic and odd as Ruth.

"Ruth, it feels as if the more I come over, the larger your house gets," I joked.

She giggled in response, blushing. "At this point, I wouldn't know. I barely spend time out of my room. There hasn't been much of a reason to leave," she whispered. My eyes went wide at her comment.

I walked over to the ballroom, unsure of how to respond to her remark. "Maybe find someone to settle down with. A husband or a roommate; I don't want you to be lonely."

"Walter, you of all people should know that marriage does not cure loneliness."

I quickly looked over at her, feeling my palms grow sweaty. I chose to ignore her comment, stepping into the ballroom.

Immediately I began grinning, looking at the three strangers that stood in the center of the room. "Am I the last to arrive?" I questioned. Ruth nodded, causing my grin only to widen. The fewer guests there were, the better the stories.

A tall, Asian man perked up and pointed toward Ruth. "Alas, the hostess returns, and with a man, I presume. How scandalous!" He was flamboyant, and it was obvious he made no effort to hide it. I quickly took notice of his curly black hair and his dimples.

"Nothing of the sort, Yuuto. This is only my friend Walter. Walter, this is Yuuto."

I walked over to the man to shake his hand, but instead, he lifted my hand to his lips and kissed it.

"Ruth, you never mentioned this Walter fellow to be so handsome."

Ruth laughed and lightly shoved his arm. "Yes I did. You asked, and I told you he was."

"But, Ruth, you said so in such a dull manner, how was I ever meant to believe you?" He winked at me and stepped away, smirking.

Next to Yuuto stood a man in a long, red, loose dress. He wore a curled, blonde wig and red lipstick. "This is Father Joseph. She is the priest of the town's only church." I examined her skeptically, unsure of how to approach her.

"Do not fear, my child. I promise I don't bite." She walked over to me and gave me a comforting hug. "Ruth has told me so much about you; it's a pleasure to finally put a face to a name."

Ruth took my arm and led me over to the final guest; she had her hands intertwined as she nervously tapped her feet. A strand of her brown hair covered half of her face, not allowing me to read her expression. "Ethel — is it Ethel?" Ruth asked. The girl nodded and looked up, loosening her muscles slightly at the sound of Ruth's voice. "Wonderful. Walter, this is Ethel. She's the sweetest and purest being you'll ever come to meet. Now, Ethel, push your hair back, darling. You have a beautiful face — the world glooms whenever you hide it." Ethel pushed her hair back and slightly lifted her chin, finally making eye contact with me. "Will Liza be joining us today?" Ruth whispered.

"Maybe later. She's very excited to see you again, as am I." Ethel's voice was small and soft, something I hadn't expected.

"I'm so glad you could all come. Apologies if you expected there to be more people today, but know it was for a good reason. Today is a very special day for me, so I wanted to spend it with my four favorite people. Five, if you'd like to count our sweet Eddie who is setting up the dining room as we speak," Ruth exclaimed as if she were speaking to a room full of eager guests.

Joseph whipped her hair back and slightly lifted her hand. "Pardon me, Ruth, but what makes today so special?"

Ruth took in a sharp breath, curling her right hand into a fist. She let out a soft laugh and whispered, "It's a surprise. Now, let's have so much fun it'll be the death of us."

"Oh, Ruth, you know I love nothing more than surprises! I simply can't wait!" Yuuto clapped giddily.

Ruth sighed, smiling. "If you all don't mind, please head to the dining room. Eddie must have finished setting up by now. I'll join you all momentarily." As everyone began to head out, Ruth grabbed my arm and pulled me back. "Wait one second. I have to talk to you." She waited for everyone to leave before offering me a seat on a sofa against a wall.

"Walter, is there anything you'd like to tell me?" she said, her voice shaking.

I blinked rapidly, my chest feeling light. "Pardon?"

She forced a laugh and began twiddling her fingers. Once she looked up and noticed my staring, she quickly stopped and sat up straight. "Well I just—who knows when we'll see each other again after the party, and I . . . I wanted to know if there's anything you wanted to say."

I chuckled. "We'll see each other again, Ruth."

She grabbed my hands and bit her bottom lip, her eyes watering as she looked up at me desperately. "Walter please. What—what if we don't? Isn't there anything you want to say to me? Anything at all?"

"Nothing you don't already know."

"Walter! For God's sake, please! Just say something!" she said desperately.

I pulled my hands away and stood, watching as she covered her face and wept.

I opened my mouth to say something but decided against it. I had never seen her in such a dreadful state, and I was unsure of what to do. "Walter, say something nice. I don't want you to remember me this way."

I sighed. "You're the most wonderful person I know, Ruth, and the happiest. I have never met anyone as bright as you and I—" My voice cracked. "We will see each other again, I promise. I will always come back." I lifted her face and dried her tears, hugging her tightly. "You're my only true friend."

Without hesitation, she wrapped her arms tightly around me, laughing. "Happy. Am I really the happiest person you know, Walter? How sad," she whispered. She then pulled away and sighed. "Sorry, that was improper. Thank you, Walter. I'm very happy I got to know you. I wish you had gotten to know me as well."

I furrowed my eyebrows, leaning against the sofa. "Whatever do you mean? Ruth, you're worrying me. Are you feeling well?"

Ruth nodded, standing up. "Yes I-I simply need a moment alone. Sorry about that. Thank you, Walter. Please head to the dining room and tell everyone I'll be there momentarily."

I examined Ruth's state, unsure if I should truly leave her. "As you wish, Ruth. Please join us soon." I took her right hand and kissed it, squeezing it before letting her go.

"I'm so glad I got to see you again." She blushed.

I grinned. "As am I."

As I left, I continuously looked back toward Ruth, watching as she sat still on the sofa. I could tell she was scared, no, terrified. It didn't feel right to leave her, but I knew Ruth always knew what was best. Whatever it was that she was terrified of, she did not want me to know. *Ruth's word is law; she asked me to leave; therefore I shall.*

I shut the ballroom doors behind me and proceeded into the dining room, where only Yuuto sat.

"If it isn't the man of the hour. Did Ruth need anything?" he asked, lifting his legs onto the table.

"She wanted to catch up with me privately, that's all. I haven't seen her in years, so there was much to say. Did I take long?"

Yuuto crossed his right leg over his left and shook his head, leaning back into his chair. He stared intently at me, not answering.

"You could fall," I warned.

Yuuto flashed a smirk. "I already have," he flirted. I snorted, looking around the room. "Our darling Ethel went to the ladies' room, and Joseph is in the kitchen with Eddie. They'll return in a bit I'm sure." Just as he finished his sentence, Ethel shuffled into the room. Her hair was put up in a french braid, and a flower had been tucked into the back of her ear.

"My, what a lovely lady you are, Ethel! Ruth was right: you are absolutely stunning!" Yuuto exclaimed, sitting up properly.

"Thank you, Yuuto. You're far too kind." Ethel blushed. She took a seat next to him. "Walter, you'll sit to the right of Ruth. She requested so before you arrived, though I'm sure she told you herself."

"I'm afraid she didn't. Thank you." I smiled, still standing.

A heavy silence fell upon the room like a wool blanket, which was unusual for one of Ruth's parties. With so many abnormal stories and traits to speak of, there was never a quiet minute that went by. "Why were you invited?" I spat, realizing after how rudely the question had been phrased.

Yuuto, however, didn't mind at all. "I think my reasoning is more than obvious: my family immigrated from Japan to Canada, which is where I was born. Then I resettled from Canada to America once my parents kicked me out for having relations with men. For my first few years in America, I made a living from selling opium and other fancy drugs, though that business got very dull after some time, so now I run a liquor store. Ruth, bless her, took me in for some time while I set up my business. She was the first person ever to see me as more than a homosexual or an immigrant, and I'll never thank her enough for it."

Ethel grinned. "I feel the same way. I'm unsure how, but though I am one body, there are two beings in me, including myself. I am Ethel, the rightful owner of this body, but there is also Liza, who joined me when I turned sixteen. Liza is thirty-four. Ruth has taken care of Liza and me many times, respectfully treating us both as different people. She also helped us learn to function together peacefully. No one has ever done so before."

"Ruth's always been accepting of everything," I said. "A pale man could knock on her door tomorrow and claim to be a vampire and she'd love him all the same. She's so understanding and accepting, it's almost dangerous." Yuuto and Ethel nodded.

Suddenly, there was a soft knock on the kitchen door as Eddie walked in. My heart dropped once I realized who Eddie really was. "Mr. Walter N. Grover, it's certainly a pleasure to finally meet you!" He reached out his hand and firmly shook mine, leaving me speechless.

"Former governor Edward Lee Alton. I am honored to make your acquaintance, sir."

"Don't be silly, boy, I'm but a mere butler, at your full service. Those days are behind me, I'm afraid; Alton or Eddie will suit me just fine."

I grinned and took a seat, shaking my head. Leave it to Ruth not only to befriend bizarre people but also to make them part of her staff as well. "Per your request, I shall call you Alton. Though your governing days are behind you, I could never feel comfortable calling such a magnificent politician by a pet name. You have my utmost respect."

Eddie blushed, nodding. "Thank you Mr. Walter, though I promise I have no problem with being called Eddie. I'm not a slave. I chose to be a butler. You may treat me as such."

"Where's Father Joseph, Eddie darling?" Yuuto questioned. He pulled out a cigar from his jacket's pocket, but before he could light it Ethel snatched it and handed it over to Eddie.

Eddie held the cigar with disgust. "I'm afraid I haven't seen her since she arrived. I thought she would be here with you. Could she have gone to the powder room?"

Ethel shook her head. "Not possible, I was just there, and I was alone. I saw her going into the kitchen."

Yuuto stood from his seat, leaving the dining room. "Yes, she told me she was looking for Eddie, though I suppose he must have stepped out when she went in. I'll look for her then."

"I'll go with him," I offered once Yuuto had left the room. I ran across the main entrance, thinking of where Yuuto may have gone. "Yuuto?" I called out, but no one responded.

No one that I thought would, at least.

"Pardon me, I'm looking for Ruth? The door was open, so I thought to come in since nobody stood outdoors. I'm terribly sorry for my tardiness." A tall Aboriginal woman wearing a white pantsuit with a belt blushed, reaching out a gloved hand toward me. "The name is Alex. I'm a guest of Miss Ruth's." I couldn't help but smile at her Australian accent.

"Walter, and as am I. I'll take you to her," I said, forgetting the reason I had left the dining room in the first place.

She took my arm and followed me into the ballroom. Though as I opened the ballroom doors I was greeted by a blood-curdling scream. Alex sprang into action, ripping a dagger from her belt. She held it out before her, ready to attack whatever had caused the chilling cry.

"Ruth! Oh heavens, Yuuto, don't look!" I heard Father Joseph exclaim. I stepped further into the room, searching for the cause of the commotion.

Then I saw her.

Ruth's eyes were wide but calm, her arm dangling off the sofa. She lay still, her magnificent yellow dress which once radiated warmth and love now battered in red. Alex dropped to her knees, the dagger tumbling off her fingers, and I looked away. I looked toward the ballroom doors with the sudden urge to sprint out of them; out of this house, out of this town, out of this world.

"Ruth."

Yuuto's whisper said it all. She was gone.

A fit of sudden anger bubbled up toward my throat. It wasn't until I was on my hands and knees that I realized it wasn't anger, but puke. "Everyone, *please,* calm yourselves! This is no time for panic!" Father Joseph screamed, though it was obvious she wasn't even composed herself.

As if to be the cherry on the bloody cake, Eddie and Ethel entered the room, only to find the terrible sight of Ruth's corpse. Ethel howled in agony as Eddie immediately wrapped his arms around her. A terrible silence fell upon us, though this time it was justified.

Chapter Two:

The Worst Hostess of All Time

Even though I had just barfed out my breakfast and lunch, I felt heavier than ever. I carried a gruesome weight.

My best friend had been murdered, and without knowing, I had known it would happen all along.

Our conversation raced through my head, leaving nothing but guilt behind. *Isn't there anything you'd like to say to me?* she had asked. *Anything at all?*

She knew. She knew everything.

"Can someone . . . take a look at her?" Ethel asked, looking at me. My stomach churned. I lifted my chin and slowly walked over to the sofa, traumatized by the sight.

Two stab wounds: one in her chest, and the other in her intestines. A shiver ran through my body as I got closer to her. "The chest wound is deeper. That's the one that killed her." I looked around the couch and gulped. "There is no weapon in her hands, so she was murdered," I further established. Yuuto released a loud sob. "The blood is . . . the blood in the stomach wound is practically dry, but the chest wound is still wet and warm. She was stabbed below her liver about fifteen or twenty minutes before she was murdered."

"Couldn't the first wound have killed her?" Alex asked. Yuuto shot her an ugly look.

"It is unlikely. A stab to the intestines is not instantly fatal; it would have taken hours or days for her to die from it."

Alex crossed her arms and stood next to me, looming over Ruth. I could tell she was trying not to cry out in anguish. "So—so someone stabbed her, realized she wasn't dead, then killed her off twenty minutes later?"

"Have decency!" Yuuto screamed, finally standing. Father Joseph grabbed his arms, holding Yuuto up. "You!" Yuuto growled, pointing to Alex. "Who the hell are you?" he choked.

Alex turned to face the rest of the group. "I'm Alex, one of Ruth's friends. We met on one of her trips to Australia." Yuuto glared at the dagger Alex had dropped, wondering the same thing as the rest of us. "I-" Alex gasped, her hands shaking. "No! I just got here. Walter saw me come in!"

My heart dropped. "I'm terribly sorry, Alex, but I saw you at the entrance. I never saw you arrive. You even told me you hadn't seen anyone yet."

Alex began to panic and made her way toward the ballroom door. However, once I realized this I sprinted into action and grabbed her arms. "Alex, I want to believe you, but you'll only seem guiltier if you try to leave. I know it wasn't you," I lied. She stood still. "Ladies and gentlemen, there's no use in pointing fingers. There is a killer among us, and by panicking we're only giving them a chance to strike again. We have to figure out where everyone was in the past hour or so."

"Can't we simply call the authorities?" Eddie asked.

"I *am* the authorities, Alton. I'm a detective," I snapped. "Let us go into another room. Ruth wouldn't want us lingering over her while we discuss her murder."

"Ruth said you were going to be an opera singer," Ethel mumbled.

"*Let's go*," I hissed, knowing it wasn't the time to swoon over my impossible dreams. The group moved along to the kitchen, which I swiftly examined. For a single butler, the kitchen was far too large; however, if anyone were to enter or leave the room, they would have been easily noticed. "I need everyone to tell me where they have been in the past hour. I know all of you have been alone at least once. Hold nothing back, for it could spare you."

"Wonderful, I've always dreamt of being interrogated," Yuuto said sarcastically.

"You sold illegal drugs, Yuuto. You must have known this day would come," Ethel said. Yuuto dropped his chin in surprise and humphed.

"Ethel, Yuuto, now is most certainly not the time for your pointless bickering. I say we do as Walter says since he *has* dealt with these types of situations before. Haven't you, Walter?" Eddie said.

My hands clammed up. The only murder case I had ever solved was one from Agatha Christie's novels. I decided not to point this out. "Of course. None of us would be here if Ruth hadn't trusted us. Therefore we have no reason to hide from each other. We must bring her killer to justice," I announced. The rest of the group nodded.

Yuuto still didn't seem convinced. "Walter you are most certainly a . . . *lovely* man, but I hate to be the one to remind us all that you were the last person known to be with Ruth."

My chest dropped. "I would never kill her," I said, my face filled with rage.

"Neither would we," he argued, smirking. "And even if we would, we wouldn't say so out loud. I say you tell us what you were talking about with her, and I'll trust you."

I curled my hands into fists, holding back the urge to tackle Yuuto. "My conversation with Ruth is mine and mine alone. I didn't know at the time, but that was the last time I would hear her voice, and I do not need to share our discussion with you to prove anything. I don't need you to trust me, Yuuto. I will do whatever it takes to find her killer. *Whatever. It. Takes*," I hissed.

Alex reached over and grabbed both my hands. "I didn't even have the chance to say hello. I'll help however I can, mate. I'm with you."

"As am I," said Ethel.

"And I," said Eddie.

"In Ruth's honor," said Father Joseph. I smiled. Yuuto slouched on a chair and crossed his arms, reminding me of a fussy toddler.

"Well then, I'd like to speak with Alton privately. We can talk in the living room," I said. Eddie straightened his coat and followed me out of the room.

We made our way into the ballroom, avoiding any visual contact with the corpse. At the end of the room stood a dull door, which Eddie gladly opened for me. I smiled, making my way into the room.

The living room was by far the weirdest room in the whole house; most likely because it didn't exist before Ruth bought it. The room was hidden away in the back of the house since it was entirely made of wood. She refused to use marble (the material used for the rest of the house) because in her words the odd difference "made the room all the more beautiful." Her usual guests did not enjoy this corner of the house and would avoid it; however, when she was alone she'd spend the majority of her time there, appreciating its quirkiness and peculiarity.

It hadn't occurred to me that now no one would appreciate it the way Ruth did, and it would most likely be torn down for its "ugliness."

"Alton, please take a seat." I motioned to one of the green sofas in the room. I sat on the sofa directly in front of him.

"We could make tea if you'd like," Eddie offered. I shook my head no. "Ruth recently added a stove to the room so she could make herself tea while she read. She dreaded getting up and having to walk to the front of the house, and she never wanted to ask me to make it for her."

I asked him why he decided to become a butler.

"I've never thought of myself as a leader. The reason I enjoyed being governor was that I was able to serve; however, it was overwhelming. Once I resigned, I still wanted to serve but on a smaller scale. I figured the best job for me was being a butler, but being the former governor and not having the proper skills made finding a job rather difficult."

"Until Ruth," I whispered.

He smiled. "Until Ruth, yes. Even now I don't understand why she hired me. I can't do much. Yet she still appreciated whatever I could do for her, so I was happy."

I grinned. "She always put others' happiness first. She hired you to make you smile, not to serve her. Though I'm sure she was grateful for the times you prepared her tea or made her bed as well." I felt my hand twitch as I spoke.

Am I really the happiest person you know, Walter?

My chest tightened.

"Is . . . something wrong, Walter?" Eddie softly asked. I snapped out of my thoughts and nodded.

"Not at all, I was simply thinking. Now, to the more basic questions. Was there anyone who may have disliked Ruth? I know it may seem improbable, but there must have been someone."

Eddie stood still for a second. "No," he answered coldly. "It was impossible not to like her. Everyone who knew her loved her."

I wish you had gotten to know me as well.

I quickly jumped to my feet. "Was there anyone you'd say she was closest to? Anyone she heavily admired? I know she's never had lovers, but any close friends maybe?"

Eddie smiled. "Other than you, she spoke highly of no one else. I'd say every week she would think about inviting you over. I doubt there was a day where she didn't say your name at least once."

I asked if he was certain there wasn't anyone else, having a strong feeling that Eddie was hiding something.

"No one else, I'm afraid." He sighed, though this time it was quite obvious he was lying. I stared at him for a bit until I decided he wouldn't tell me whatever it was he was hiding.

"Alton, where were you when Father Joseph went into the kitchen? Ethel said she saw Father Joseph go in; however, you said you never saw or heard her do so. Therefore you couldn't have been in there."

Eddie stared at me, unfazed by my observation. "She may have gone in while I stepped out. I was in the wine cellar for some time before returning to the kitchen. I'm afraid I have no one to verify it, but I promise it's true. However, promises don't help you much, do they?"

I hadn't realized he had asked me a question. I chose not to answer. "Well then, there's nothing else I'd like to ask for now. Could you bring Father Joseph in for me?" I asked. Eddie nodded and left.

Moments after his departure, my stomach churned with the realization that I was completely alone; I cursed under my breath and tried to stare at the ground until Father Joseph arrived. However, I knew my mind would find something to entertain me with. *"Playing detective yet again?"*

I looked up.

And there She was.

I chuckled to myself. "Did you expect any different?" I responded. She sat down in front of me, placing Her hands over Her lap. *"Let me help you this time. Don't shut me out."* I snorted. *"You have to trust someone,"* She argued. "Trusting you wouldn't count, since you aren't real," I countered.

"May I come in?" Joseph asked, opening the door. I stood and gestured toward the sofa in front of me, welcoming her into the room. Joseph sat next to Her.

"Thank you for coming down. Do you mind if I ask an off-topic question?"

"Since I was seventeen," she quickly responded.

"Pardon?"

"I've known I was a girl since I was seventeen. Isn't that what you were going to ask? My sister wore the most lovely dress to our aunt's wedding, and I wanted to try it on the entire time. During the ceremony, she and I snuck out of the church and hid inside the restaurant a party would be held in afterward. We sat in the wine cellar where we stole some rum and just giggled away, gossiping with one another. Then I asked if we could switch clothes. She laughed when she saw me in the dress. She thought it was all a silly joke; I felt reborn." Joseph sat up proudly. I looked to the imaginary person sitting next to her, but She was looking out the window as Joseph spoke. "Ever since then I've wondered what I'd change my name to, what it would be like to be entirely female; but what's the point of encouraging what cannot be? No one would accept a transgender priest."

"Will you resign? *Can* you resign?" I asked.

"Depends."

"If you could, would you?"

"I don't know." She shrugged. I nodded.

"I apologize if I was prying. Ruth always invites people with the most wonderful stories, and I couldn't help but ask for yours. It's the least I could do on Ruth's behalf."

"There's no need to be sorry, my child. Curiosity is not a sin. Now on with the questions."

I nodded. "When you went into the kitchen, did you see Alton?"

Joseph shook her head.

"This may be odd but, did you see any wine by any chance?"

Joseph giggled. "That is quite a peculiar question. I don't recall, but I do know Eddie had pulled out a bottle of something before you arrived. He had said he was going into the wine cellar, and Yuuto insisted on going with him since he wanted to get a drink. He came back with two or three bottles, I think."

"And Yuuto?"

"He held one, which he kept to himself."

I frowned. "I don't remember him having a wine bottle with him when I came in."

"He must have set it down somewhere. May I ask why this is important?"

I shook my head and told her she could not. "Where were you before you went into the kitchen?"

"The library, wandering. I'm positive Ethel saw me leave the room when she was going to the bathroom."

"You saw her going into the restroom?"

"I did. Does that give her an alibi?"

I shrugged. I could think of nothing else to ask her, so I told her she could leave.

"Do you want me to bring someone in?" Joseph asked.

"The Australian girl. She seems exciting," She offered. I ignored her and smiled toward Joseph. "No, I'll go out with you. I want to examine Ruth again." I took Joseph's arm and walked out of the room with her, hoping She would stay behind. *"But I'm a part of you, Walter dear. You can't abandon your thoughts,"* She mocked. "I can sure as hell try," I muttered.

Father Joseph's eyes widened at my comment, but she chose not to question me. I was immediately thankful she hadn't.

Joseph quickly pulled away from me once we entered the ballroom. Without even excusing herself, she sprinted along the walls of the room and yanked the doors to the entrance open, jumping out as soon as she could without even saying goodbye.

"Terrible manners, that girl. She ran away without even looking back; reminds me of someone I know," She criticized. She clicked Her tongue while She lingered above Ruth's corpse. *"The body seems colder than before. What a horrible sight."* I moved over to Ruth, feeling my stomach churning. *"You don't have to do this,"* She sang, taunting me. "I don't, but I will. She was my best friend." I snapped, kneeling down to get a closer look. I suddenly felt the urge to bawl my eyes out, but I decided against it. *"Your best friend? Are you certain of that?"* I jumped to my feet and faced Her, glaring into Her nonexistent eyes. "I don't care how many secrets she hid from me, or how many lies she may have told. She loved me. She loved me in a way you never

could," I growled as hot tears boiled my eyes. *"Then why'd you marry me instead of her?"*

I picked up a strand of Ruth's red hair. I let it curl around my fingers, then watched her hair slip away from my grasp. She seemed far too calm to have been brutally murdered. "You knew." I chuckled, looking over at the wounds. "You hadn't invited me to one of your parties in years, Ruth. I wondered why you suddenly insisted I come. Now I know." I gently lifted her dangling arm and placed it just below her lower wound. "You wanted me to solve your murder." I sighed and examined the sofa, searching for any broken glass.

"What are you looking for?" Ethel's soft voice somehow echoed around the room.

I looked over to her, examining her face. Her expression was different.

"A weapon, or whatever it was that killed her," I mumbled.

Ethel slowly walked over to me, blinking rapidly. Her left hand was shaking, but she didn't seem to mind it. "I want to see her. I want to see what happened."

"But haven't you already? Ethel, I think it's best not to look."

"I'm not Ethel," she corrected. "I'm Liza. And I want to see Ruth for myself."

I nodded and stepped away, examining Liza's face. She sat next to Ruth and stared at her as if trying to convince herself that it was a hoax and Ruth would sit up at any second, assuring everyone she was fine. "She looks peaceful," Liza noticed. I nodded. "Do you think she knew?"

I choked at her assumption. "Why would she?" I asked, sitting next to Liza. I continued to look around the sofa for any clues.

"She looks too calm for it to have been a surprise. I'm no expert, but it also doesn't seem like she struggled to fight back. Besides, she seemed a bit down the last time I saw her. She's been nervous and hasn't left her house in some time. I even arrived early to make sure she was feeling better," Liza whispered, staring at Ruth's hair.

"When did you see her last?" I asked, looking under the sofa.

"I think a week or two ago. She asked me to try to come as myself, not Ethel."

"How come?"

"I'm not sure," she answered hesitantly.

I pretended not to notice. "You're easier to talk to, it seems. More confident, and older," I noted. Liza smiled. "Is that why you came along? To help Ethel be more sure of herself?"

"I suppose you could say so, yes. I see potential in Ethel, and she just needs someone to help her along. She needed someone older to give her advice and support her, so that's what I became. Someone she can go to for comfort and reassurance."

I smiled. "How were you able to meet Ruth as yourself and not Ethel? Can you control when you switch?"

"I come when needed, and whenever Ethel is willing for me to step forward."

"That's wonderful," I complimented. "Now, I'm sorry, but did Ruth say anything to you when you saw her? Anything . . . I don't know, odd?"

Liza froze for a second, pondering my question. "Her enthusiasm felt forced, as if it were an act she had to uphold. She was also quite jumpy, I suppose; she was always startled by the smallest movements. She was on guard every minute I spent with her, and according to Eddie, she began to feel this way after receiving a letter. I'm sure Eddie mentioned it to you."

I clenched my fists. "He didn't. I'll speak with Alton afterward. Could you help me for a moment and inspect the sofa for any shards of glass? Even the smallest piece is enough."

Liza shook her head. "Pardon me, but I'd prefer not to help you. I'm terribly clumsy, and I'm afraid to touch or do something that may impact your deductions. Besides, I'd rather go back and mingle with the others since I haven't seen many of them in some time. I only came to see Ruth, and you."

I waved her off and continued to inspect the surroundings, feeling disappointed but understanding her reasoning. I wouldn't want to be around Ruth's corpse for so long either; however, it appeared to be what Ruth desired of me. I stood, scratching my head. There was no sign of broken glass anywhere near the sofa, so it couldn't have been a glass bottle, though the wounds seemed to have been made by a thin, sharp object. I turned around and noticed She wasn't there. "So you appear only when you wish, I see. Fine then. Be that way," I pouted aloud. I rapidly examined the rest of the ballroom, looking for any sight of glass anywhere. "Could have been broken somewhere else. Yuuto couldn't have downed the whole drink and not be drunk, so he must have done something to that wretched wine bottle," I muttered to myself. I remembered Yuuto with his cigar and clicked my tongue. I noted his smoking and possible drinking habit and decided to ask about it later.

I stood up and made my way toward the library, which was in the next room. As I entered, I was immediately overcome with the smell of smoke. I instantly knew who it was.

"Yuuto, your time is up. Throw the damned thing out." Eddie rolled his eyes, taking the cigar from Yuuto's lips.

"Thank the heavens. I couldn't stand the smell," Alex groaned, swatting at the air. Joseph coughed, glaring at Yuuto. Yuuto, however, stared intently at me as he let out his last puff of smoke.

He walked toward me, grinning. "Forgive me, Detective, but I couldn't resist. I am but an addict." He reached forward and straightened my blazer. I looked behind Yuuto and smirked at Joseph.

"I'm afraid you're asking the wrong person for forgiveness," I teased. "Who gave him permission to smoke?"

Eddie raised his hand. "We all consented to it. Liza said you were in the ballroom, so we gave him permission to smoke until you came back."

I chuckled. "Then I apologize for taking so long; if I had known I would have hurried." Everyone smiled, and for a moment we forgot about the heavy anguish bestowed upon us minutes ago. "Alton, would it be odd to ask for dinner? I'm completely starved, and I would like to speak with you all." Eddie blinked twice before giving a hesitant nod.

"If that is what you wish. The dining room is prepared, so if you could all make your way into the dining room and sit in your corresponding seats while I fetch tonight's meal, I'd be more than grateful." Eddie quickly scuttered out of the living room, all of us slowly walking behind.

I looked behind me and saw Joseph whisper something into Liza's ear, causing her to stop walking. Joseph pushed her hair back and quickened her pace. Once Liza noticed my staring, she began walking again, pretending nothing had happened. She tightened her hands as she walked past me, knowing I would ask her about the interaction eventually.

"Do we all remember where to sit?" Yuuto asked once we had all entered the dining room.

I stared at my seat, the one that would have been next to Ruth, and I gulped. Chills ran up my spine as I was the first one to be seated, nodding to the others as if to give them permission to do the same. Everyone slowly took a seat, visibly uncomfortable.

I lifted my hand as I circled my index finger around the rim of the wine glass before me, wondering if it would be improper to ask Yuuto about the wine bottle. "Will you check her room?" Liza asked.

My head shot up from the glass. "Possibly. You mentioned something about a letter, correct?"

Liza tensed, fumbling with her hands. "Y-yes, I did. Though I'd rather you not disclose anything I've told you unless positively necessary. I don't want to be the next victim because I chose to tell you the truth."

My face flushed and I looked around the table, watching Yuuto hold back a smile. "Of course, I understand. I'm sorry," I apologized, and waited for Eddie to return.

"Pardon me, but Eddie is alone," Alex stated, standing by the doorway. Everyone's eyes widened as we realized what that meant.

Almost immediately, I sprung to my feet and ran into the kitchen, searching for Eddie, who loomed over the stove. "Don't move!" I exclaimed, causing Eddie to yelp and drop to his knees. The rest of the group clambered into the room, overwhelming Eddie. "Alex, check the sink and make sure there are no knives or sharp objects. If there are, see if they are wet. Liza, make sure Alex doesn't hide anything. And, Alton, don't be ridiculous, and stand up,

41

you're alright for now." Alex and Liza walked over to the counters, examining the kitchen sink.

"Nothing here," Alex announced, looking toward me. Liza nodded as to confirm the statement.

"Very well then. I'd like for someone to test all of the food in case something has been poisoned; after all, we're not sure if the killer is satisfied just yet," I suggested. The group's eyes went wide.

"I'll do it. I've tested food several times during my travels," Alex offered, giving Eddie an apologetic look. "I'm sure all of your cooking is magnificent, Eddie, but we wouldn't want it to be the death of anyone."

The kitchen door opened yet again, revealing a smug Yuuto. I felt my breath hitch as I realized he didn't enter the kitchen with the rest of the group. "Ruth once said you were very trusting of others, Walter, though quite frankly I have no idea where she got the idea from," he joked. "No one would dare lay a finger on Eddie's cooking without him allowing it. His meals are sacred, and no one with a sane mind would meddle with them."

"What part of 'there's a killer among us' do you not seem to understand, Yuuto? No one with a sane mind would mess with Eddie's food, but we are not dealing with someone who holds a sane mind. I'm trying the food just in case," Alex insisted, moving to my side. Yuuto sneered and leaned onto the doorway, rolling his eyes.

"Oh, hush, if anything you're most likely the killer. You held a dagger when you walked in, for God's sake!" Yuuto exclaimed, causing Joseph to gasp. "Sorry, forgot you were here, *Father*."

Eddie fumbled with his sleeves as he presented the feast he had made before Alex. "Yuuto, it's alright, please no fighting or accusations, not in my kitchen," he whispered, watching as Alex gulped and began tasting the meals, hesitating afterward, expecting to fall dead any second.

Alex sighed after tasting the last dish. "It all tastes amazing, Eddie. I'm impressed. Even better since nothing killed me." No one laughed.

Eddie began shoving everyone out of the kitchen, telling us to wait at the dining table. "You're a scoundrel, Walter," Yuuto hissed beneath his breath. He leaned into me, his lips barely touching my left ear. "You expect us to trust you when you won't even trust one of us to leave the group for a mere second without a crime being committed?"

"Careful, Yuuto, I don't believe you're the one to speak since you were, or are, a criminal yourself," I warned, stepping away from him. He huffed as he sat down, placing his chin on his right hand. Everyone made their way to their chairs, waiting for my next words.

"Alex, where will you be sitting?" Liza asked. Yuuto and I quickly made eye contact and turned to Alex. There was a seat for everyone that was meant to arrive at the party, but they were one seat short.

"Were you supposed to come?" Yuuto stole my question.

"Of course, Ruth invited me. I can even show you the invitation if you'd like," she began, shakily pulling out a piece of paper from her boot. I reached forward and scanned it, determining the handwriting to have been Ruth's. I reached back and gently grabbed Alex's hand, standing.

"While we wait for Alton to prepare everything, I'd like to speak with you outside. You wouldn't mind, would you?" Alex shook her head and made her way out of the room.

As soon as Alex had stepped out, all eyes were on me. I gave them all reassuring smiles as if I was entirely sure of what I was doing. I spun around and stepped out of the dining room, shutting the door behind me. I pressed my left ear against the door to see if the atmosphere of the room shifted once I stepped out, but they were all silent.

"Walter, you must understand I'm not up to anything," Alex spoke from beside me, prompting me to jump away from the door. She stood eerily still as she pulled at her fingers and nibbled her bottom lip.

I stepped forward and examined her demeanor, realizing then she was on the verge of tears. "Alex, I know it wasn't you," I whispered. Her glazed eyes shot up in surprise, and her jaw dropped. I debated whether I should tell her the truth. *"Of course, because you can't allow anyone to help you, can you, darling?"* Her voice hissed at my side. Shivers ran up my spine as I quickly glanced to Her. *"Think rationally, Walter dear. Ruth knew she would be murdered; she even invited you to solve it. Look at this child, overwhelmed at the accusations. You haven't even said a word and she's already scared. Do you truly think she is capable of murder?"* I gritted my teeth and pulled Alex farther away from the dining room. "Do you mind if I examine your invitation?" I asked her. She quickly handed over the piece of paper and played with her long, curled hair.

"Walter, I don't think she wanted me here for the party; I was only a few minutes late, not long enough for a murder to occur. If you want I could even go into town and ask for the cabbie. That's a thing you can do, right?" Alex continued fumbling with her hair as she watched me read the invitation.

That's when I noticed.

"Alex, your invitation is different. Yours has a different time; the party began at five forty-five. Yours, however, says it began at six forty-five. The writing also appears to be messy, which could indicate it was written in a hurry. Where do you currently live, Alex?"

"Australia. I'm an explorer, though not a very good one. I have a deathly fear of practically everything, but I can't help but feel the need to go out and be dangerous. It's upside-down logic, but Ruth would always tell me she admired my ability to step out of my comfort zone flawlessly. Though I don't see what there is to be admired, if I may be so bold."

"Put a sock in her mouth, won't you, darling? She's not letting me focus." I gritted my teeth as I hissed out, "I don't need your help."

Alex's eyes grew wide. "Do you think that's why I'm here? To help you?" I held my breath as I heard Her snicker beside me. "But then she'd have to know she'd be murdered, wouldn't she?"

"She did," I confirmed, my voice cracking at the end. "She pulled me aside minutes before she was killed and asked me if there was anything I'd like to say to her since we may never have the chance to see each other again. I didn't know at the time . . . I thought she didn't think I'd ever come back to see her. She was shaking, looked absolutely terrified. She knew she was going to die, and she wanted me to be the last person she spoke to. She wanted me to solve her murder, and I assume she wanted you to assist me."

Alex bit her quivering lips. "Do the others know?"

I shook my head.

"Very well. I would like to help you, Walter, if you'll let me."

I smiled. "Two minds are better than one. Now, you arrived here an hour late; therefore Ruth must have known she would be killed in the first hour of her party."

"You mentioned she was scared and spoke to you knowing she would be killed at any second. That further proves she knew she would be murdered at the beginning of the party."

I nodded. "Yes, however, that's not enough evidence to prove she knew; words are quite useless, I'm afraid. But now that we have solid evidence, we can share it with the rest of the group."

Alex frowned. "I don't think so. If anything, it proves my innocence, but you'd have to explain Ruth's demeanor to come to the conclusion she wanted you to solve the murder. And even now, that's still a hypothesis."

"Not if she left something behind to prove it. Ruth was smart; she must have left something for me. I know she would."

Before Alex could speak any more, Eddie peeked out from the dining room and into the entrance. "Pardon, but dinner is served."

Chapter Three:

Revelations Come with Consequences

"Ugh, I thought we almost solved it. This is dreadful!" Yuuto whined. I smirked and snuck Alex's invitation into my blazer pocket.

We had all gathered in the library. Joseph and Eddie stood in a corner, while Yuuto sat on the seat closest to me, his left leg hung off of the arm of the sofa. Liza and Alex sat in front of me, both looking equally exhausted.

"Yuuto, that is terrible manners. At least we have canceled out one of the suspects, meaning Walter is closer to ending this nightmare," Eddie reassured, smiling to me. Yuuto sighed and stood up, massaging his forehead before looking to me.

"I'm sorry, but we shouldn't forget that now that we've cleared Alex's name, Walter is now the greatest suspect. He said the first stab wound occurred twenty minutes before her actual death, and who was the last to see her? How do we know Walter wasn't the one who stabbed her?" Yuuto accused. His voice was soft and filled with sadness. "Walter, please clear your name," he insisted, his eyes glowing with captured tears. "I don't know about the rest of you, but I have had enough of this. Ruth didn't deserve to die the way she did. She's done so much for all of us, and I can't believe someone thought the best way to pay her back for her kindness was to kill her. Imagine all of the lives she could have helped, how she could have changed the world." Yuuto took a deep breath as Joseph burst out sobbing, and Liza hiccuped as she prevented herself from breaking down. Yuuto leaned forward and took my hands in his, gulping. "Walter, you're our only hope. There is a monster among us, and Ruth needs you to find them. *I* need you to find them, please. Defend yourself."

I blinked rapidly at Yuuto's words. His expression was serious and firm, a look he hadn't worn that evening. I licked my lips and examined the expectant faces that waited on me. "I-" My throat dried up and I choked. "I couldn't have committed the murder. I was with you in the dining room," I recalled.

"You were with me during the supposed time of Ruth's first wound, but then we left to look for Joseph, which according to you, was around the time Ruth was killed," Yuuto countered.

I sighed in frustration. "If you really need proof I wasn't involved in any way, I know how I can declare my innocence," I offered.

Yuuto gave in to a small smile. "Then do it."

I opened another drawer, taking in a deep breath to calm the anxiety that vibrated through my arms. I was kneeling before Ruth's dresser, praying she had left something behind in my favor. *"That's if she's as smart as you think she is."* She hissed from behind me. I chose to ignore Her.

"Is there any way I can help, Walter?" Eddie asked from the doorway. The group watched me intensely as I scavenged through Ruth's room.

"Afraid not, Alton. It's something I must find myself." This statement was untrue, though no one questioned it.

I pulled away from the drawer and examined the disorganized room. Papers were messily scattered around her writing desk, and books were piled on both of her bedside tables; her bed was neatly made, but on the edge of the bed was a box of unnecessary objects Ruth most likely didn't know what to do with. The room was just as untidy as I had pictured, knowing she wasn't keen on order. I gulped and thought deeply about the kind of person Ruth was, hoping that would give me some sort of clue. "I can't find it. I've looked in all the likely places." I admitted. Everyone shifted uncomfortably.

"But what is it that you're looking for?" Alex asked from the door.

"I don't know, but I know there's something." I groaned. I ran my fingers through my hair anxiously as my brain whirred for answers.

That's when it hit me.

I wish you had gotten to know me as well.

"Oh!" I exclaimed, causing the group to jump back. "Alton, what other room are you not allowed to clean?"

"Pardon me?" He asked, surprised by the question.

53

"Clearly she didn't allow you to clean her room, that's why it's a mess; however, you were allowed to enter because the bed is made, and Ruth doesn't bother closing her drawers after opening them or put her clothes away after wearing them, so why would she make her bed?" I beamed with pride. "You weren't allowed to clean her room; it's a mess, but one she understands. Now, what other room were you not allowed to clean?"

Yuuto smirked as Eddie stuttered, shocked at my deduction. "The guest bedroom at the end of the hall on the right. Though she banned me from entering it entirely, had a key for it and everything."

"Where is it?" I asked anxiously.

"I'm afraid I don't know, but I could look for-"

"No, she didn't want you entering it for a reason so she wouldn't hide it anywhere you'd search," I stated, watching as Eddie's teeth grit in annoyance. I looked around the room once more, looking for any tidy places. *"Oh please Walter, even I know where it is. Ruth was preparing for her death weeks before the party began, so she must have hidden it somewhere safe, not unlikely."* I stared at Her and grinned. "Of course. Liza?"

Liza grimaced. "Yes?"

"You've done well; please hand over the key," I said, holding out my hand. I waited for her to move, hoping I was correct and not making a fool of myself.

Liza stepped forward, sitting on the edge of the bed and taking off her right shoe. She turned it over, and the key fell from her shoe and onto the ground, its presence stunning the guests. I smiled and hugged Liza tightly, feeling her sniffle onto my shoulder. "She wanted to see you, Liza," I began, pulling her away and grabbing the key, "because she knew you could keep her secret safe. Ethel can come back now."

Liza stared down with a plain expression before shivering and suddenly slumping and smiling shyly. Ethel reached forward and hugged me before getting up and standing by the door with the rest.

"How the *hell* did you figure that out?" Alex asked, immediately receiving a nudge from Joseph.

"I spoke to Liza while I was examining Ruth," I explained, "And she told me she only shows herself when she is needed and when Ethel is willing to switch; Liza presented herself to me shortly after I finished interrogating, and began talking to me about Ruth and the last time they spoke. When I asked why Ruth had wanted to speak to Liza, she hesitated in her response. I assumed whatever Ruth had told her had to be kept secret. Ruth was preparing for her death, so she had to give the key to someone she knew would keep it safe after her death, and that was Liza, a confident, trustworthy woman who resides in Ethel and only appears when necessary."

Ethel grinned. "Liza and I had no idea why she gave us the key, but she was desperate for us to take it. Said to keep it safe, so Liza put it in my shoe."

"Why didn't you bring this up earlier?" Joseph asked.

"Ruth said to keep it hidden until it had to be given up."

I reached over and kissed her forehead, walking away from her and heading to the room. "She would be proud, Ethel."

The group watched from Ruth's room as I placed the key into the doorknob and slowly twisted it open. The door unlocked, and I motioned Alex to follow me into the room.

As I stepped in, I was overcome with the smell of lavender. I looked around, surprised at how neat the room was. There was a queen-sized bed on the far left corner covered in blue silk, and next to it was a white lowboy dresser with perfumes and jewelry placed on top. The walls of the room were covered in large paintings with price tags hanging from them. Finally, a shaker writing desk stood parallel to the dresser, and on it was an envelope. I looked around the empty, expensive room before making my way toward the envelope I hoped was for me.

"This looks far too luxurious for Ruth. She was a humble woman. She wouldn't buy so many . . . costly things," Alex mumbled from the door.

"That's what she would have liked us to believe. She lived in a mansion. It makes far more sense for her not to have been as humble as she seemed."

"But really, look at all of these paintings, the jewelry; and the perfumes, most of them unused! What would be the point of buying these things if she never put them to use?" Alex asked, irritated.

I smirked, picking up the envelope. "There is no feeling like that of mindlessly spending money." I ripped it open as Alex stared at me gawk-eyed. I pulled out a piece of paper, noticing both sides were filled with writing. "This is it," I whispered. "Alex, please go keep an eye on the others." She nodded and left me alone.

"They're coming for me, Walter, and there's nothing I can do about it.

I'm assuming that if you're the one reading this, then I'm dead. I'm also assuming you've figured out by now that I knew this was inevitable. I would have told you I knew of this, but I couldn't risk putting you in any danger, not when you're the one I need the most. Think of this as my final request, though I'm certain that won't be enough reason for you to do as I ask, no matter how much you care for me. Trust me when I say this is for the best. Mr. Walter N. Grover, I need you to find my killer and protect them."

I stopped to read the line again, not believing my eyes. *Protect them*? *Protect her killer*?

"I have invited the people I deem are more likely to murder me, though there's a possibility I was wrong.

Please keep this in consideration in case all the guests lead

to dead ends. Once you find my killer, bury me in my

garden and act as if I wasn't real. Any and all

documentation of my existence has been destroyed.

Therefore my disappearance will be far more believable.

Do not tell the rest of the group about this. Finally, I have

written on the back the names of people I know couldn't

have killed me, including you. These people were invited

so they may assist you in your investigation. DO NOT take

them for granted.

Solve my murder, Walter, and follow my requests.

These are my dying wishes. I love you, and I'm terribly

sorry you must see me as I am."

I felt my throat dry up as I turned the paper

around, examining the short list of innocent names Ruth

had left behind. I quickly looked around the room once

more before walking out and locking the door behind me.

"Where's the letter she received?" She asked from behind me.

I turned to look at Her and frowned, examining the room

and reminding myself to look later. "I have names," I

announced, leaving the room. The group stood in the hall,

tensing at my words. "Ruth has left behind a list of names

composed of people she has stated are innocent and did not kill her."

"Don't say them, please," Eddie spat. My eyes went wide at the statement.

"Why?" I asked cautiously.

He stepped forward before he responded. "It'll cause disruption. We're all friends here, and knowing these names may cause arguments and chaos. Wouldn't it be better to keep it to yourself? That way we can all stand in harmony."

Yuuto snorted. "As *kind* as your comment is, I'd rather know who is and isn't trustworthy. Besides, we'll figure it out eventually anyway, since Walter will probably go to those on the list for assistance." Eddie smirked and stared at Yuuto. "Moreover, what are you afraid of, Eddie? Got something to hide?"

Eddie's jaw dropped at the accusation. "Yuuto, I am *not* hiding anything, and this is exactly what I'm talking about! We have to stick together in order to find this killer, and arguments like these will only make Walter's job harder. If we all mingle peacefully among each other, then Walter won't have to worry about solving more than one murder!"

"Quiet!" I spat. "The list only affirms my suspicions. I won't read the names, but I assure you mine is one of them."

"Why should we believe you so easily? Can't we see?" Father Joseph demanded.

"I have never been invited to one of Ruth's parties before, and I'm her best friend. Why would she suddenly invite me to the party at which she is killed?" I said. "I'm a detective, and she knew she would die today. That should be enough reason to trust me."

Yuuto stepped forward, eyeing me suspiciously before nodding and facing the group. "Ladies and gentlemen, it's getting late, and the only reason we're any closer to understanding what has occurred so far is due to Walter's skills, so I suggest we *shut up* and do as he says."

Ethel stepped forward. "Now then, Walter, what would you like for us to do?"

"I'll head to the living room. I want to continue the interrogations. Alex, I'd like for you to take everyone back to the library. Keep an eye on things while I'm gone."

"Who will you interrogate first?" Alex asked.

I shrugged. "No one in specific. Is there anyone who'd like to be first?"

"I'll come," Yuuto volunteered. I nodded.

"Alright then. Everyone, relax for a bit. I know it's hard, but it is my job to find the murderer, not yours. Yuuto, follow me." Everyone walked out of the hall and down the stairs until the group disbanded from Yuuto and me. Finally, we entered the living room and Yuuto carefully sat before me.

"Eager?" I joked. He smiled nervously before fumbling with his hands.

"It's better to get this over with sooner than later."

"You didn't think so when I first brought up the interrogations," I smirked.

"People change."

"In less than an hour?"

He chuckled, causing me to smile. "I was impressed with your deductions upstairs, how you found the room. Some of us lived here for months and didn't even give that door a second glance." I stared at him for a bit as I waited for Her to appear.

She didn't.

"Yuuto, you spoke earlier about your admiration for Ruth. Would you consider yourself to be closer to her than the rest of the group?"

Yuuto relaxed. "Well . . . maybe, I think so. I lived here for a long time. It took me about six or seven months to get back on my feet. Eddie took care of me during that time, while Ruth helped me find a place and a job I'd enjoy."

I raised an eyebrow. "Alton took care of you?"

Yuuto's face went bright red. "I—yes, he, of course, made the meals and taught me how to clean and cook. God knows I wouldn't be able to afford someone to do all that for me."

"Were you close to him?"

"I don't want to talk about my relations with the people in this house."

"And yet you're talking about your relationship with Ruth. You've already revealed part of your secret, why not reveal the rest?"

Yuuto smirked as he crossed his left leg over his right. "That was clever." He shook his head and examined my face. "Why do you want to know?"

It was my turn to smirk. "If you were, or are, it could be useful. Besides, I already know the answer, Yuuto, but I'd rather you admit it so I may proceed with the questioning."

"I was. Not so much now."

"How come?"

Yuuto's smile faded as his expression shifted. "He and I had . . . a bit of a dalliance. It was short and meaningless, though it gravely upset Ruth. She let me stay, but for a long time, I thought I'd be out on the streets. She somehow forgave me and let me stay for two more months before I knew I'd outstayed my welcome. Although it really was meaningless."

I leaned forward. "Did that upset you?"

Yuuto gulped. "I don't see what that has to do with Ruth dying."

I shook my head. "Sorry, you're right," I said. "Why did it upset Ruth?"

"Well, Eddie wanted to keep it a secret, which was understandable; however, Ruth had opened up to me so much during the time I was with her, and I had done the same. We were both close, yet I was keeping this ridiculous secret from her . . ." Yuuto looked down at his hands, unfolding them. "Eddie told her. Couldn't hold back the guilt any longer, though I distinctly remember he told her it meant nothing and *I* was the one who wanted it to be secret. She was devastated, insulted I didn't tell her. I never got the chance to tell her he lied."

I frowned. "Why didn't you tell her then?"

"She wouldn't have believed me," he snarled. "Why would she? My word against her *precious* Eddie's would have been worthless anyway."

"She would have understood—"

"No, Walter, she wouldn't have. You didn't know her as I did," he hissed. "I loved her dearly, but she is not who she claimed to be. I peeked into her room once, the secret one. She draped herself in jewels and expensive scarves as she wildly danced to her record player, *smoking*. I've seen her angry too, throwing things around her bedroom as if the devil were there to take her soul, screaming like she was possessed. There were sides of her that no one will ever know about, and quite frankly, I'm glad. She was magnificent, and she deserves to be remembered the way she presented herself."

My hands tensed as I looked away from Yuuto's stern expression. "What was she really like?" I asked.

He smiled softly as he leaned closer to me. "Walter, you may not have been by her side for many years, but she spoke of you like a brother. The love and compassion she held for you could never be properly expressed, but I assure you, it was great." He slowly reached for my hand, waiting for me to flinch. I didn't. "I can see why now. I'm sorry I spoke ill of her and Eddie, but it was a rough time, one I'm obviously bitter about." He moved in closer, causing my breath to hitch. "And I assure you, even though the Ruth you knew was a lie, her love for you was true." He glanced down at my lips before smiling reassuringly.

"Yuuto, I'd like for you to leave," I declared, turning around.

Yuuto frowned and blinked rapidly in bewilderment. "Walter, I'm sorry I—"

"*Get out,*" I hissed. He left without another word.

As the door shut behind him, my hands reached for my lips, gulping at the thought of Yuuto being so close. "*The nerve that man has,*" She tsked. My head shot up as I glared at the figure sitting where Yuuto once was. "*I think we can both agree he has quite the motive, wouldn't you agree, darling? Such a sad, sad man.*" "Shut up!" I yelled, pulling at my hair. His eyes had been shining with *something*, hope perhaps? I recalled the way my breath stopped as he grew closer, his eyes glimmering.

She scoffed as She looked to the door. "*I can't believe this. You'll really settle for anything, won't you?*" I grinned. "Well, I married you, didn't I?" Her smirk dropped as She stood up, walking to the windows. "*Get the next one. I can't stand being in the same room as you for so long, not when there's nothing entertaining.*"

A knock.

"It appears someone heard you," I mumbled, but She was gone. I rolled my eyes and gave the visitor permission to enter.

Ethel shuffled into the room, her left hand hidden behind her back. "Walter, I'm so sorry," she whispered. I frowned.

"Ethel, what are you holding?" I questioned. She looked up to me before sniffling.

She slowly moved her left hand forward, revealing the object in her hand. My eyes grew wide. "It can't be . . ."

Chapter Four:

Confessions of a Married Man

Yuuto sat before me and the group, which had migrated to the living room. I held the broken wine bottle in my hands, grabbing it by the neck. The bottom half of the bottle was missing, pointed shards left as evidence that it had been shattered.

"Please, you have to believe me, Walter," Yuuto begged softly, staring at the broken bottle in my hands. "I didn't break it. I put it away once I had enough. I didn't want to get drunk, so I left it on the counter for Eddie to do as he pleased. Eddie, tell him!"

I looked at Eddie, who stood silently. "Alton, can you testify?" I asked. He shook his head.

Yuuto sprang to his feet, his eyes bloodshot and puffy. "Lies! That's all you ever do, isn't it, Eddie? First, you lie to Ruth, and now, you're framing me for my own friend's *murder*?" Yuuto's voice cracked. He stepped forward and spat at Eddie. Eddie's eyebrows furrowed as he jabbed at Yuuto's jaw.

"Stop it! Stop this!" Ethel screamed, pulling Eddie away. I quickly moved to Yuuto's side as he crumbled to the ground.

My word against her precious Eddie's would have been worthless anyway.

My heart raced as I stared at Yuuto while he gripped my arms. "Yuuto is innocent until we can find the rest of the bottle. It is possible someone took the bottle and broke it in order to make him appear to be the culprit." Yuuto's tired eyes examined my face as I spoke.

"I'll look for it," Eddie offered.

"No, Alex will. Alton, stay here with the rest of us. I don't trust you to wander about by yourself," I retorted, frowning. "Yuuto, are you bleeding?"

Yuuto dabbed at his chin with his fingers, shaking his head after a quick inspection. "It doesn't seem like it. It didn't hurt much anyway, just caught me by surprise." He forced a half smile as he chuckled.

I helped him onto the sofa and sat next to him. "Alex, I'll stay here. Search the library and the kitchen.

Come back when you're done." Alex saluted as she left the room. I turned to Ethel, who was whispering something into Eddie's ear as he glared at Yuuto. "Alton, stand as far away from Yuuto as possible, please." I looked to Joseph, who stood by the windows, playing with a strand of her hair. I frowned as I noticed how unphased she appeared. "Father Joseph, are you alright?"

She quickly looked up and nodded. "Oh, yes, of course. I just think it's better not to speak, as doing so seems to be starting fights." She glared at Eddie before looking away. "All of these accusations and secrets are exhausting, and it's almost eight thirty. Will we be allowed to return to our hotels or homes?"

"I'm afraid not. There are four guest rooms if any of us wish to sleep, since it is much safer to continue the investigation with all of us here."

Joseph frowned. "Will *you* sleep, Walter?"

I smiled and shook my head no. "Most likely not. But don't worry about me. As I said before, I'd prefer you all calm down and leave this situation to me."

71

Joseph snorted at my suggestion. "Walter, I'm afraid that is easier said than done. You are not the only one eager to understand what has happened."

"And he's aware," Yuuto began huskily, "but this is his kind way of saying we're idiots and better off out of his way unless he specifically asks us to contribute."

I snorted, and the rest of the guests smiled.

"And for the record, Eddie," Yuuto continued, "if I get a bruise because of your stupidity, I'll slaughter you. I take very good care of my appearance, and I'd hate for it to be ruined due to your petty blow."

Joseph grunted at Yuuto's comment. "Yuuto, I believe *slaughter* is not an appropriate word to use in your case. May I remind you that you are being accused of murder?"

Yuuto lifted his chin and raised the corners of his lips. "I'll remind *you* I'm not the only one."

I rolled my eyes and shoved him. "Yuuto, do me the favor of shutting up," I mumbled, and he smiled. Eddie huffed as he turned around, continuing his quiet conversation with Ethel. Yuuto sniffled next to me, looking over toward Joseph every so often. "Yuuto, how long have you been smoking and drinking?"

He shrugged. "I can't recall, maybe since my teenage years. If you think I developed my habits due to my professional past, you're wrong."

"Have you ever considered quitting?"

"The thought has come to mind, but it isn't appealing. Maybe in the future. My turn to ask an uncomfortable question: how long have you been with your wife?"

I tensed. "Almost a year, I think, I don't remember."

He laughed. "Ruth said you were married longer; how bad of a husband are you?"

"Not a good one. And it really has been about a year. I was married before Helen; that must be why Ruth said I'd been married for a long time."

Yuuto pulled himself away as his eyebrows furrowed together. Ethel and Eddie's whispering came to a sudden halt as they attempted to eavesdrop. "My first wife left me, ran away with her secret girlfriend."

Yuuto grinned. "You don't seem too upset by it."

"It was a shock at first, but I always knew she wasn't interested in me. Though I proposed anyway since her father wouldn't stop blabbing about what a wonderful pair we'd make. I'm glad I was able to get him off of her back." In mere seconds, I felt Her looming over me. *"Oh, I'll kill you, Walter, because we both know you are the least heroic being in the tale of our pathetic love story."*

"What about Helen?" Ethel asked from the corner, unashamed of her eavesdropping.

"Are you going to pretend she's a lesbian too?" She said bitterly. I gritted my teeth at Her snide remark. "I met her a few months after my divorce. It was at a bar I think, and I invited her for a walk. We went out for a good six months before I popped the question. Her only goals in life are to marry and have children, so she didn't hesitate with her answer." I chuckled. "Though shortly after the wedding, it was as if she was an entirely different person; everything she had claimed to love, she hated, and confessed she hadn't enjoyed many of our dates. She promised to be her true self now that we're married and spends all of her time trying to be the perfect wife."

"That sounds dreadful," Yuuto complained.

"Yuuto's right, that sounds awful. Why don't you divorce her? She only wants to use you, not love you," Eddie agreed.

Joseph shook her head. "It would ruin her. All she wants to be is the perfect housewife. Imagine how she'd feel if she found out she failed? True, what she did was inconsiderate, but she would never get the chance to achieve her desire to settle down with a family if Walter were to leave her."

I nodded. "She's so passionate about family, I couldn't do that to her." I shifted as I heard Her hiss behind me, *"You mean your conscience wouldn't be able to handle it."* My breath stopped. *"You're pathetic, Walter. You marry women you don't love, and you don't think twice about the people you hurt along the way. But you'll never tell these people that, will you?"* She strolled to Yuuto's side, examining him. She stroked his cheek, and I felt my chest tighten. *"I'm leaving. This stopped being fun some time ago. But let it be clear: I pity Helen, and now I pity Yuuto, for entering the curse that is loving you."* I watched as She dissolved, leaving me alone with my regrets.

"Walter?" Joseph asked. I picked my head up. "I asked for your first wife's name."

"Oh," I began, "her name was Ruby."

Ethel smiled. "That's a beautiful name. What was she like?"

Before I could say anything, Yuuto stretched out his arms and yawned loudly. "Goodness me, how long does it take to find the bottom half of a bottle? It feels like it's been ages."

"Be patient, it hasn't been long," Joseph said. I looked to Yuuto and nodded thankfully.

Ethel and Eddie went back to whispering, while Joseph continued to gaze out the window. As I looked around the room, I felt Yuuto slip his hand into mine and squeeze it. "You're welcome," he whispered, before standing and reaching for a cigar in his pocket. "Do you mind?" he asked, waving the cigar before me. I shrugged.

"Not at all. Though ask the others first. I'm going to go check on Alex." I quickly stood up and began to walk out of the room, before I felt Yuuto grab my shoulder.

"Are you leaving me in charge? Please leave me in charge."

I laughed, opening the door. "You're in charge."
Yuuto beamed as I stepped out, beginning my search for
Alex.

I quickly walked through the ballroom, ignoring
Ruth's decomposing corpse on the couch. As I opened the
doors that led to the entrance, I saw the front doors open.
"Walter?" a woman called out. I frowned as I noticed it
lacked an accent.

"Alex?" I asked, hoping it was her. Once the
stranger stepped into view, my body froze in place.

Helen stepped inside, gripping the large fur coat
that hung from her shoulders. "Walter, there you are!
Who's Alex?"

Helen sat on a counter in the kitchen, drinking a
glass of water as she watched me pace back and forth in
front of her. "Helen, you shouldn't have come," I stated.

"I know, it's the fifth time you said so," Helen
pouted, taking another long sip of her water. "Are you the
only one who stayed after the party?"

"Yes, I offered to help clean up," I mumbled,
fumbling with my blazer sleeves.

Helen nodded. "Can I meet Ruth then?"

I choked as I shook my head furiously, taking the glass of water from her hands. "N-no, she's busy cleaning up. I wouldn't distract her," I stuttered, almost dropping the glass. "Besides, she doesn't feel well, and meeting someone new will require energy she doesn't have, and I just want her to relax."

Helen raised her right eyebrow but thankfully believed my lie. "Why shouldn't I have come? You said the party would be over at quarter past eight, so I came to make sure you were well, like a good wife should."

I shook my head, ignoring her growing smile. "You should have waited for me to call. Besides you shouldn't just walk into a house like that, it's impolite."

"You said she welcomed anyone, and the door was open."

"But it's morally incorrect to just waltz into anyone's house. You should have knocked," I hissed. Helen's smile dropped as she slipped off the counter. "Go back to the hotel, won't you? I'm going to stay here tonight to make sure Ruth sleeps well. She really is very ill."

"Then why didn't the party end early if the host is so sick?" Helen argued.

I turned my head, thinking of a fast excuse. "Ruth insisted the party should continue."

"That's terribly irresponsible of a hostess."

"It doesn't matter now. I must stay and make sure she is taken care of."

Helen wrapped her arms around me and kissed me, beaming. "You're such a kind person, Walter, but I'm sure she can manage by herself. Doesn't she have a butler?"

Before I could respond with another lie, Alex burst through the kitchen, holding the bottom half of the bottle. My eyes went wide as I motioned frantically at her to leave, but rather, she stood by the door, baffled. Helen turned to look at Alex, letting go of me as my heart dropped.

"Hello! You must be Ruth!" Helen exclaimed, walking over and shaking Alex's hand. Alex looked to me, waiting for instructions.

"Ruth! Wh-what are you doing back here? I told you to wait for me in the living room since you don't feel well," I stuttered, hoping Alex would tag along.

Alex let go of Helen's hand and frowned, attempting to process the situation. ". . . Right. Sorry, but you were taking your time and I wanted to check up on you. Who is this?" she asked, quick to understand.

I sighed. "This is my wife, Helen. I'm terribly sorry, but she came to check in on me since the party ended and I wasn't at the hotel. Though I explained to her I'm staying to make sure you're well."

"Of course," Alex started, "my butler is currently on leave, so I'm home alone. I needed a helping hand since I'm not feeling too well, and Walter being the angel he is decided to stay and assist me. You've married a wonderful man."

Helen nodded, smiling toward me. "I most certainly have. Anyway, if you'd like I wouldn't mind staying and helping as well—"

"No, that's alright. We have it all under control. Is there anything you need?" I interrupted. Alex nodded in agreement, fumbling with her belt, trying to keep her dagger out of view.

"No, I think I'm alright. Our chauffeur, Charles, is outside waiting for me, and I've checked in, so all is well. Though I don't mean to pry, why are you holding that glass?"

"Oh someone broke a bottle and we couldn't find the other half, but I did so it's all fine. Would you like for me to walk you out?" Alex answered, dropping off the broken glass and taking Helen's hand, dragging her out of the kitchen before Helen could respond.

I sighed and slumped onto the counter behind me, massaging my head as I waited for Alex to come back. I leaned forward and slowly walked over to the broken bottle, picking it up and examining it. There were bits of dirt spread around the bottle, showing it had been hidden outside or in one of the potted plants. The bottle was a dark green. However, no signs of wine or blood were anywhere on the bottle. "Your wife asks too many questions," Alex joked, stepping into the kitchen. I looked up from the bottle and chuckled. "I found it outside, next to some trash bins. There didn't seem to be any stains other than the dirt."

I raised the bottle to my nose. "It smells like soap and dirt, but there's a lingering smell of wine, meaning it was washed but not well."

"Washed in a rush maybe?"

I nodded. "Most probably. And considering that it smells like soap, whoever put it outside didn't even attempt to wash off the detergent, so they were in quite the rush. And not long ago, either, since the smell is still a bit strong."

Alex frowned. "But how could someone break and hide the bottle without any of us hearing it?" I shrugged and began to walk out of the kitchen, Alex walking beside me.

"We should hurry, the group has been alone for too long."

Chapter Five:

As the Water Begins to Boil

Alex held the body of the bottle as I placed the neck onto it, making sure no large pieces were missing. "It seems to fit well enough. There are a few shards missing, but nothing that could be used as a weapon. If it was Yuuto, he didn't use the bottle."

Yuuto scoffed as he tapped my back. "How kindly put, Walter. Now may we worry about truly concerning things such as the fact that the murderer is now *framing* guests?"

"Yuuto's right. We need to make sure that any clues we find from now on are valid and not tricks planted by the murderer to distract Walter," Alex agreed.

"Is there anything we can do to help?" Joseph asked sincerely. "We could work as a jury perhaps, whenever you find something. Maybe some other opinions could assist you."

I shook my head. "I'm afraid not. Alex will work as my second opinion, but thank you anyway. I need you all to understand that you cannot help me with this case since you are all suspects. Until your name is cleared, I'm sorry, but I cannot accept your help." The group nodded, understanding.

"If I may ask, what took you so long? You were gone for some time," Eddie asked.

Alex snickered. I pushed back my shoulders as I frowned. "Helen came to check in on me, wanted to know why I wasn't home just yet."

"Oh, I can't believe we missed that! What did you say?" Yuuto laughed. The guests began to grin as they waited for an answer.

I couldn't help but smile as the atmosphere around us lightened. "I said Ruth wasn't feeling well, so I stayed back to give her a hand with things and make sure she is sound. Alex came in as I was talking to her, and Helen thought she was Ruth." The group chuckled at the story, some throwing their heads back in laughter.

"That's terrifying! And she didn't see through your lies?" Ethel giggled.

Alex piped up, "No! It was bloody awful. She kept asking questions I didn't have the answers to. I'm surprised she believed anything I had to say."

The laughter died down as the jokes came to a halt, though the smiles remained plastered upon everyone's faces. "This is what Ruth would have wanted, for us to enjoy ourselves, not wallow in sadness. Why else would she call this a party?" Eddie spoke up.

I smiled. "Alton, you're absolutely right."

"But what about the case?" Joseph asked.

I shrugged. "I'll continue looking, but yet again it is my job to worry over this, not yours. Enjoy yourselves."

"In that case then, I'd like to get some sleep if I may. It's been a long day, and truly, I need the rest severely." Joseph chuckled.

"I'd like to get some sleep too if that's alright," Ethel chimed in. Eddie nodded in agreement.

I nodded. "It's settled then; we'll head upstairs. Alex, if you don't mind, could you guard the halls while everyone's in their rooms? Only to make sure no one tries to pull anything."

"No worries, I reckon I could stay up all night if need be. I'm not used to the time change just yet," Alex reassured.

"Before we leave, though, Alton, do you by any chance remember a letter Ruth received some time ago?" I quickly asked. Eddie frowned.

"A letter?" he mumbled.

"I was told she got a letter that upset her. Do you know where it might be?"

Eddie's eyes widened as he revived the memory. "Right! That letter, yes, it would most likely be in her room. After reading it she asked me not to throw it out."

I thanked him as we headed out of the living room, scuttling through the ballroom.

"Ethel, is there any chance I can speak to Liza? Or could you pass along a question for me?" I whispered as we made our way out of the room. Ethel nodded.

"I could try. What do you need?"

"Could you ask her what it was that Father Joseph whispered to her? It seemed to bother her, and I wanted to make sure she was alright."

Ethel thought to herself for a moment before looking back to me, frowning. "You're terrible at hiding things." I stopped walking. "That's what Joseph said."

"Where's Joseph?" I asked, looking around the group.

"She's up there," Eddie called from the bottom of the stairway, pointing to the top of the steps. I ran up the stairs and stood next to her, walking the rest of the way up.

"Goodness, what's wrong?" she asked, yawning.

"How did you know about the key?"

Joseph blinked once. Twice. Finally, she took a deep breath and looked behind us before answering, "I didn't know about the key. But I know Liza well enough, and when she's as quiet as she was then, it means she's lying or hiding something. And due to the way she stopped, I knew I was right." Her voice lowered as she leaned in closer to my ear. "Walter, I know I have no clear evidence, but I'm almost convinced she's the murderer. Consider what I've told you, won't you?"

I looked down the stairs, watching the group talk amongst themselves and occasionally smile. I noticed Alex glancing up at me worriedly but not interfering. "I will," I whispered, standing at the head of the stairs and waiting for the rest of the guests to catch up. "Alton, if you don't mind, could you sleep in one of the guest rooms tonight? It would be easier to have everyone in the same space."

Eddie nodded. "Of course, I understand. However, there are only four guest rooms and there are five of us. One of us would need to double up."

I raised my hand. "I won't be sleeping much, so I don't mind sharing a room with someone."

The group was silent, eyes wandering each other. "I can share a room with you since I'll be keeping watch outside, so I won't sleep much either." Alex smiled. I nodded.

"Perfect. Everyone should have a room then. Ladies and gentlemen, there are clothes in each guestroom if you are interested in changing out of your attire. As you all know, Ruth has a habit of inviting strangers into her home, so all of the rooms are filled with the necessities you may require. If there is anything else you need I will be more than pleased to assist." Eddie looked over to me. "Walter? Anything you'd like to say?"

I nodded. "Goodnight."

The group smiled as they all made their way into different rooms, closing the doors behind them.

"I'll pull a chair out of Ruth's room and sit outside. Will you need anything?" Alex asked.

"Not at the moment. I asked all the questions I needed to before they headed off. I'm going to look around Ruth's secret room to see if there's anything else she left behind."

Alex nodded, heading to Ruth's bedroom. "Walter," she said, looking up to me, "who were the other names on the list?"

I walked toward her, leaning into her ear. I carefully whispered the names, stepping back and turning so that I wouldn't see her reaction. "That doesn't leave many suspects," she said plainly.

"No, it does not."

"Walter, have you already solved the case?"

I shrugged. "I have my assumptions. Though there is still much I must find in order to confirm my suspicions."

"Do all detectives work this quickly?" Alex joked, leaning against the doorway. I turned to face her, the edges of my lips lifting slightly. I examined her stance before looking away and taking out the key to the secret room. She chuckled. "Walter, promise me that if you do not follow your dream of singing you'll at least make a name for yourself some other way. You are incredibly gifted, and though I haven't heard you sing, I reckon you're as good as they get. You deserve to be remembered."

I squeezed the key in my hand, my chest growing tight at her words. I closed my eyes and imagined Ruth standing behind me, waiting for an answer. "I promise," I murmured, unlocking the secret room as Alex stepped into Ruth's bedroom.

My lungs were overcome once more by the smell of lavender as the door opened. "Ruth, what did you use?" I muttered, looking around the room. I surveyed the room, venturing to identify the smell's source. Eventually, I stopped before the closet doors and pulled them open. I stared at the record player before me and noticed a shelf above filled with lavender scented candles, five which were burning. I coughed at the smell as I pulled them down, blowing out the lights. "Why light so many? Why *have* so many?" I wondered aloud. I placed the candles back on the shelf and closed the closet doors, beginning to look around the room. As I opened the drawers of the lowboy dresser, I noticed one filled with cigarettes and scribbled papers. I watched the cigarettes roll off the papers as I pulled them out, examining the writing. "This could be of use," I muttered. I closed the drawer and sat on the bed, organizing the sheets before me.

"What's that?" a soft voice questioned from the doorway. I looked up to see Yuuto, who was still wearing his normal clothes.

"Aren't you going to change?"

"Would you like me to?" he teased.

I snickered. "I found these in one of the drawers of the dresser over there," I said. "I'm not sure if they'll be helpful, but they might be."

Yuuto stepped into the room, looming before me. "You should sleep instead, so you can have more energy tomorrow and solve the case quickly."

"Why are you in such a rush to get this over with, Yuuto?"

I heard him stutter. "Shouldn't we all be? Once again, my friend's corpse is downstairs and her killer is sleeping soundly in one of her rooms. Do I need a better reason?" I didn't respond, knowing he had a point. "I came here to apologize, about earlier. I didn't mean to insult you or offend you in any way. It's not in my place to speak of your relationship with Ruth, and I should have realized it's still a sensitive subject."

I felt my cheeks flush at his words, a nervous sweat forming at the top of my forehead. "I'm sorry I overreacted. I've heard so much praise on Ruth's behalf that hearing someone speak poorly of her upset me. I should have been kinder." I swallowed as I felt my throat growing dry. Yuuto chuckled as he knelt down and pulled me into a hug, resting his chin on my shoulder.

"All's forgiven, Walter. There's no need to be sorry." He assured me, squeezing my arms before pulling away.

"I do have a question for you," I remembered. "You said before you have seen Ruth dancing with scarves in this room, didn't you?"

"Yes."

"Why didn't you mention the fact that she had a secret room then?"

Yuuto giggled, taking a seat next to me. "I like observing you as you work, it's entertaining. Besides, I had no idea it would be important."

"You didn't think a *secret room* would be important to this case?"

"Why would I? I'm not the detective here."

I snorted, shaking my head. "That's incredibly suspicious, Yuuto."

"But you already know it wasn't me, don't you?"

I didn't answer. Instead, I fumbled with the papers, pretending to examine them. "You don't really believe it was me, do you, Walter?" Yuuto asked again, his voice deeper and more serious than before.

"Yuuto, everyone is a suspect. I can't cross you out simply because I think you're—" I stopped my sentence, laughing. *"Charming,"* She finished.

Yuuto stood up, unamused. "My name wasn't on the list, was it? That's why you're doubting me."

"Yuuto, I can't—" I started, reaching for his arm.

Yuuto jerked away, lifting his hands in disgust. "Amazing. Absolutely amazing how terribly cruel Ruth could be, isn't it?" Yuuto lifted his chin as he stared at the ceiling, blinking back tears. "I'll tell you something, Walter, and I don't care if this makes me seem guilty, but Ruth was *not* a good person. It was all a facade, a play she put on to entertain herself. A show she put on for *you* because it was always about you. It was her constantly wanting to impress you, to make you believe she was an angel from the heavens! Of course she cared about us, there's no doubt about that, but she didn't do it to help us; she did it to make herself feel better. Because I'll tell you something, Walter, something no one in this house has the courage to say." He stormed close to me, his face inches away from mine. "She may have been pretty, but she was terribly *rotten* inside." Yuuto stepped away, heading toward the door.

"You idiot, don't let him get away. Not this one."

"Yuuto!" I exclaimed, turning him around and pulling him into a hug. I felt his arms grow tense before relaxing onto me. "I want to believe it wasn't you. Trust me, I want nothing more than to know you're innocent."

Yuuto wrapped his arms around me, suddenly sobbing onto my shoulder. I pulled my head away and kissed his cheek, tightening my hold. "I need you to do me a favor, Yuuto." I let go of Yuuto and smiled, brushing the tears from his face. "I need you to tell me what she was like."

"Yuuto, wake up. It's one in the afternoon," Someone cooed, tapping Yuuto's shoulders. He yawned before opening one of his eyes, staring at the person in front of him.

"Let me sleep all day, Ruth, I beg you."

The red-haired woman giggled, tugging at the blankets on Yuuto and exposing him to the cold climate. Yuuto cursed under his breath before curling up into a ball and moaning. "Have mercy, please."

Ruth giggled as she opened the curtains. "Yuuto, I have to meet someone today, so I need you wide awake to help Eddie in case he needs anything. Could you do that for me?" Ruth asked.

Yuuto sat up and yawned, nodding. *"You don't need to ask twice, Ruth,"* he murmured, sliding out of bed and stretching. *"Who are you seeing?"*

Ruth clenched her fists as she looked out the window, turning to face Yuuto. *"Someone. Though if anyone asks, tell them I've gone shopping. Do you understand?"* Yuuto frowned at the sudden change in Ruth's voice.

"Alright, may I ask why?"

"Just do it, Yuuto, please."

Yuuto opened the closet doors as he furrowed his eyebrows. *"I will. I was merely wondering. You're not in any trouble, are you?"*

Ruth slammed her right hand against the window, her cheeks red as she turned to face Yuuto. *"I'm fine, Yuuto. Drop it and get dressed."*

Yuuto bit the inside of his cheeks as Ruth stepped out, his heart aching as she closed the door behind her. *"Damn it, Ruth, why won't you talk?"* he mumbled under his breath. Ever since Eddie had confessed to Ruth, her demeanor had changed immensely around him, causing him to feel guilty over something he didn't do. Yuuto quickly picked out an outfit and threw it on the bed before running out into the hall, searching for

Ruth. "Ruth!" he screamed, waiting for a response. Suddenly, he heard the faint sound of a record player at the end of the hall. "Ruth?" he asked again, walking toward the room. He pushed the door open slightly, peeked in, and gasped at the sight.

Ruth was draped in jewels and scarves, spinning around her room in a short-sleeved dress made of red linen. She came to a sudden stop as she looked out the window, waving to the outside. "I'm coming down now! Go to the front!" she hollered, taking off the jewelry and throwing it onto the bed. She picked up the wide skirt of the dress and made her way across the room, revealing her golden slippers. Yuuto jumped away from the door and tip-toed back to his room once he realized Ruth was leaving. As he slipped into his room, he heard Ruth come to a stop.

"Yuuto?" she called out.

Yuuto instantly jumped onto the bed, his heart beating fast. "Yes, Ruth?"

"I'd like to apologize for my outburst. I haven't been very kind these past few months, and I realize this now. I hope you will forgive me."

Yuuto smiled as he placed his head on a pillow. "There's nothing to apologize for. I'm only glad we were able to see past this situation. Thank you for everything you've done."

"It is my pleasure, Yuuto."

Yuuto heard Ruth walk away, leaving him lying alone on his bed. After several minutes he slowly rose up, looking out the window as he saw Ruth step out in her red dress and hug a man that waited by a car. Yuuto began to open the window, planning to greet the stranger —

Then Ruth leaned forward and pressed a kiss onto the man's lips.

"An affair?" I whispered.

Yuuto shrugged, looking over to the desk. "I assume so. I mean, she wanted me to lie about where she was, and she secretly met with this man countless times. That day a lady came and asked for Ruth, and I lied, said she had gone out to town. I could only assume it was the man's wife, girlfriend, or something. A few weeks after that, Ruth went silent; she barely spoke, only asked if you were coming. She said she had to know if you were coming so she could get ready, because she didn't want you to know something was wrong. She must have been caught."

"But you have no proof?"

Yuuto pointed to the papers in my hand. "Maybe it's there. She had to free herself from her sins somehow, and she obviously wouldn't go to church considering she knows everyone there."

I raised an eyebrow. "Free herself from her sins?"

Yuuto laughed at the statement, shrugging. "She definitely had a lot of built-up guilt and needed some kind of outlet for it. Haven't you ever done something that made you feel so bad you felt you'd explode if you didn't tell anyone?"

I squeezed my hands as I felt the right side of my lip perk up at the question. If She were here She would have laughed. "Haven't we all?"

Yuuto looked out the door and back at me, contemplating what to do next. "Do you mind if I stay? I'm not tired, and I'm incredibly bored."

I shrugged and lifted the papers. "Not at all. I hope you don't mind me working."

"Didn't we just establish the fact that I most certainly do not?"

I beamed as Yuuto shifted around the bed, lying down behind me while I read.

"I know I shouldn't see him, but I do anyway.

It isn't like I enjoy his company, because I don't.

But he enjoys mine, even though he shouldn't.

We shouldn't be doing a lot of things."

I frowned as I noticed an address scribbled on the side. *Probably his*, I concluded. I studied the paper, noticing the multiple wax stains, and a corner that had been burnt off. "It seems she tried to burn them," I noted aloud. Yuuto leaned forward, his face hovering above my shoulder.

"Maybe she didn't want anyone to find them?"

"But something changed her mind. Look at all of the papers. They're all burnt on the same edge, meaning she tried to burn them all at once but stopped."

"It's only the corner too, and not even a lot of it."

"Meaning she wasn't entirely dedicated to the idea in the first place. Just burning the corner made her regret it." I set the papers aside and looked to Yuuto. "But what changed her mind? Or more so, what encouraged her not to do it?"

Yuuto picked up one of the papers and said, "Walter, look at this one."

"The more I write, the worse I feel.

I'll die before anyone finds these, before anyone knows this is who I am."

I felt a chill run up my spine at the words. "Well, she did," Yuuto muttered, setting the paper down. "It appears she only wrote her feelings of guilt but never went into detail about what was causing it."

I reached for a lengthy written paper. "I beg to differ," I sighed, holding it up. Yuuto whistled as he nestled onto my shoulder, reaching for the paper.

He cleared his throat before holding the paper out in front of us, reading it aloud.

"I will pay for my sins soon enough. I have received a letter, one announcing my end. The worst part is that the list of those who would kill me with no hesitation is longer than one would hope. If there's one person who can prevent my death, it's Walter".

At this point Yuuto stopped reading, waiting for a reaction. I stayed silent, waiting for him to finish.

"I have planned a party, one made up entirely of those who resent me, those who would enjoy knowing about my demise. Then, Walter will be invited, and he will capture the murderer before I can be killed, and all will be well; at least, that is what I hope. If I die, I will not blame him but myself for lying. I would not be in this situation if I had only spoken the truth. Though Walter is bright, and I know he'll realize something is wrong the minute I talk to him. I refuse to be afraid of this letter. I refuse to believe I will die. I will not die. I will pay for my sins, but not on that day. I will be saved."

Yuuto dropped the paper on my lap, wrapping his arms around my shoulder. "Walter, I—" he began. "Did she say anything to you? Anything that made her situation obvious?"

I slumped into his arms, my head spinning. "Yes," I choked.

"What did she say, Walter?" he whispered. I stayed silent.

"Who knows when we'll see each other again after the party?"

"Walter?" Yuuto asked again.

"I'm very happy I got to know you."

"I didn't know she was going to die. I thought she was scared we wouldn't see each other again. I thought she was upset I didn't visit her. I thought that's what she meant when she—" My voice cracked. Yuuto squeezed my arms as I felt my body grow numb, and I recalled the last conversation I had with Ruth.

"I don't want you to remember me this way."

Chapter Six:

Paying for Our Sins

I opened my eyes, yawning. Being awake was the last thing on my list. However, the sound of a toddler crying in the next room forced me out of bed. "I'll take care of it," I mumbled, softly kissing the person sleeping next to me.

I put on my slippers and made my way out of the room, stumbling into the child's bedroom. "You're far too alert for three in the morning, little one," I joked as I picked up the baby from her bed and held her close to my chest. "Let's change you, and then we'll get you something small to eat. How does that sound?" The baby babbled in response, and I felt my lips curl up until she resumed her crying.

"I've already changed her," a hoarse voice spoke up from the doorway.

I turned around, holding the little girl.

"She's been crying all night; there's no stopping her. I think she's sick."

I looked at the baby and noticed her cheeks were a bright shade of pink, and every so often she would shake in my arms. "I'll call Thomas, see if there's anything he can offer." I left the room and picked up the phone, quickly dialing Thomas's number. After a few rings, someone finally picked up.

"Who the hell is calling at this bloody hour?"

"Hello, old chap, it's Walter."

"Walter! Is something wrong?"

"Jasmine's not well. We've never seen her this way."

There was silence on the other side. "What are her symptoms?"

"She's burning up and shaking. Hold on, Ruby has been caring for her all night, so I'm sure she has more information." I pulled my face away from the phone. "Ruby, my love! What are her symptoms?"

"She's been coughing, shaking, and is incredibly hot. Her breathing is also quick and short," Ruby called out.

I repeated the symptoms to Thomas. There was a long pause. "I'm terribly sorry, Walter. But I believe she has caught the flu."

"Can you help her?"

"I'm so sorry," Thomas whispered, *"but there is still no cure."*

"Walter, you have to get up," Yuuto cooed. My eyes shot open as I examined the room around me.

"Can't," I stated, staring at the ceiling. The memories of the night before flooded back into my mind for the second time that morning, and the urge to sleep it away grew strong once more. "I can't move."

"We're all waiting for you."

"Yuuto, I failed her," I whispered, so softly I was unsure if he had heard me. My eyes began to burn as Yuuto sat me up, hugging me.

"You didn't know she was going to die. This wasn't your fault. She should have called the police the second she received the letter, or at least told you outright what was wrong. How were you supposed to guess she was going to *die*? None of us saw it coming, so why should you have?"

"Because she expected me to," I muttered, my body growing numb again.

"Walter, I'm terribly sorry to be the one to tell you, but you are not a god. You are human, and she demanded too much of you. You have to understand that." Yuuto shifted onto the bed, allowing me to fall back onto the bed. "Come eat breakfast, Walter. Take the morning off, relax for a bit before you get back to work. A lot has happened in very little time, and you and the rest of us need a moment to process."

"When did I fall asleep?"

Yuuto smiled. "I don't recall the time, though you were crying, mumbling to yourself for some time until you fell asleep on me. I placed the papers on the desk, and I tucked you in before I got some sleep of my own."

I stretched and pushed the blankets away from me. "Where is everyone else?"

"In the dining room, waiting for you. I hope I didn't intrude," came Alex's voice from the doorway. "Yuuto said he was going to get you, but he was taking too long."

I quickly stood up, feeling faint as the blood rushed to my brain. "They can't be alone!" I gasped, stumbling off of the bed.

"Easy there, Detective. Didn't we just discuss the fact that you are not an all-knowing immortal being? Alex, go downstairs so this fool can tidy himself without having a stroke midway."

Alex giggled as she nodded and left the room, leaving Yuuto with me. He stood up to close the door, then turned to face me with his arms crossed.

"Promise me, Walter," he said sternly.

"What?" I mumbled, sitting up from my place on the floor.

"You will rest, even if it's only for an hour."

I pushed my hair back as I stood, squinting. "Why do you care about me?" I asked quietly.

Yuuto chuckled, looking down at the ground. "Because you're a good person, Walter. And you don't deserve to suffer."

"You don't know that."

"I do," he responded with certainty. I smiled, walking toward him.

"Thank you," I muttered, straightening my shirt and quickly brushing my hair with my fingers. "How do I look?"

Yuuto laughed, opening the door. "Presentable."

As we made our way into the dining room, I noticed everyone sitting around the table had dark circles under their eyes.

"It appears I wasn't the only one who had a rough night," I noted, but only Ethel smiled.

"I kept having nightmares. It was awful," Ethel said.

I looked at Alex, who sat at the end of the table, where a chair had been added. "I'm sorry I wasn't able to help last night. Were you able to sleep?" I asked her.

"I was, for a tad. Yuuto offered to take my place for some of the night and made me coffee." She smiled to Yuuto, who only nodded in response.

"You've done plenty for Walter, Alex. You deserved some time to yourself." He winked.

I laughed as I sat down, looking around the room. "Eddie should have returned with breakfast some time ago, shouldn't he have?"

Ethel stood up. "I'll ask how much longer it'll take and bring in some fruits, so we can chew on something while we wait."

As Ethel walked into the kitchen, the rest of us began to chat among ourselves, chuckling every so often. Just as things were beginning to calm, Ethel returned from the kitchen with a blank stare and empty hands.

"Where's the fruit, darling?" Yuuto asked, his eyebrows furrowing.

Ethel looked to him and suddenly began to bawl, falling to the ground as she began to shake and wheeze. I shot up from my seat and sat next to her, unsure of whether I should hold her or not.

"Ethel, look at me. I need you to look at me," I insisted.

She forced her head to turn, her breath hitching as her shaking became more violent.

"Focus on your breathing, Ethel," I cooed, performing the action with her. After a few minutes, her breathing returned to normal. The group surrounded her, scared to investigate what had caused her severe reaction. "How do you feel?"

"Help me stand," she choked, reaching out a shivering hand. Alex pulled her up, hugging her. "Walter, you have to go into the kitchen," she stuttered, hugging Alex back.

"Ethel, what happened? What did you see?"

Ethel took a quivering breath, turning to face me. "Eddie's dead."

My heart dropped. I scrambled onto my feet and burst into the kitchen, examining the room. I walked behind a counter and gagged as I saw Eddie lying on the ground, blood splattered over his chest as a knife hung from his fingers. His eyes were wide, and his mouth was open. "Where is he?" Alex choked from the doorway. She scuttered to my side and pressed her face against my arm once she caught sight. "Oh, Eddie . . ." she puffed, stifling a sob.

"He was killed. He was killed, and someone made it seem like a suicide." I sighed, growing faint.

"You two, get out of the kitchen! Now!" Yuuto exclaimed, not wanting to step into the room. Alex and I tried to move, but we both remained motionless, unable to part our eyes from the terrifying corpse.

"Joseph, help me get them out. They shouldn't be in there, it'll hurt them," Yuuto screamed. Joseph and

Yuuto ran into the kitchen and grabbed us both by our arms, dragging us out. "Sit down, I'll get water."

My hand shot out automatically as I clutched his arm. "Yuuto, don't. Stay." We both stared at my hand, still gripping him.

"Alright, I'll stay," he whispered, peeling my hand off. He led me to one of the chairs and sat me down, standing and assisting Alex and Ethel onto chairs as well. "Walter, I hate to ask at a terrible time like this, but what do you suggest we do?"

"No one can go into the kitchen, not until I examine it. Alton didn't kill himself; he was murdered. His face . . ." I shook my head. "He was killed. For those of you who are hungry, Ruth had a tea set in her living room. It's likely there are treats in there as well. Though do not go alone. Remember, Ruth is still in the ballroom, and it's a sight none of us should see, not after this. Finally, take the morning to mourn. We have lost two wonderful, inspirational souls, and we all need some time to grieve. Please remain in the library or the living room," I ordered. The group nodded, standing and shuffling out of the dining room. I stayed seated.

"What will you do?" Yuuto asked. I glanced to him and felt myself tremble.

"Yuuto, you are aware that you are the greatest suspect now," I said, rubbing my hand on the nape of my neck, softly tapping my foot against the marble ground. Yuuto pressed his lips together as he crossed his arms.

"I have an alibi. I haven't spoken to Eddie all morning," he stated, his head tilting.

"You, you could have gotten someone to kill him. Maybe you came up for me in order to distract me." I pressed my fists on the table before me, tapping my foot against the ground.

Tears formed around Yuuto's eyes. "Or I just wanted to make sure you were alright. Walter, what you're saying doesn't make any sense."

"I met you yesterday. How do I know you aren't lying or manipulating me?" I responded, feeling my chest ache. "Just because I like you doesn't mean I can just erase you as a suspect."

Yuuto sputtered, "I can't believe this. I can't believe you. Do you really blame me for this, after what I've done for you? I open my heart to you, tell you things I long to forget. I cradle you as you cry and help you sleep. I offer my assistance many times, and *this* is the conclusion you come to? I loved Ruth and Eddie, you absolute fool, and quite frankly, I am beyond insulted." Yuuto's voice rose as he spoke, shaking.

"But Yuuto—"

"I have an alibi, Walter! Why do you still want to pin this on me?"

"Your motive is strong, and you have bitter feelings for both victims. It just—it has to be you!" I yelled, my breath quickening.

Yuuto scoffed, disappointed in my explanation. "Unbelievable. You're just looking for someone to blame, aren't you? I can't believe Ruth expected you to be able to solve this case, never mind save her." His expression changed the second the words escaped his lips.

I took a deep breath and looked away, slowly pushing my chair back.

"No, wait, Walter, I shouldn't have said that. It was unnecessary. I'm—"

"Don't apologize, Yuuto. You're right. I don't understand why Ruth ever believed I could do this."

Yuuto bit his lip. "But you can. You've been doing splendidly so far. I didn't mean what I said. We're both just upset. I didn't mean it," he insisted, moving closer to me. "I'm terribly sorry. I didn't mean it."

I lifted my chin and examined Yuuto's face, lifting the corner of my lips. "Thank you, Yuuto. And I'm sorry for what I said, I just . . . wish I could have prevented Eddie's death. I wish this was all over," I admitted. Yuuto took my hand and smiled, lifting me from the chair and hugging me.

"None of this is your fault, Walter. I wish you didn't feel like you have to suffer this alone."

I sniffled and pulled away from him, offering him a half smile. "Let's forget this happened and head back with the others. Does that sound alright?"

"Perfect." He sighed, relieved.

The emptiness in my chest grew larger every day, an unimaginable pain haunting my thoughts more often than not.

"Lunch," Ruby whispered from the doorway. Her eyes were red, her hair disheveled. I slowly turned my head, examining her ghostly demeanor.

"Come sit, Ruby," I said, my voice barely above a whisper.

"I made lunch," she repeated, shuffling into the room. Her legs shivered as she sat down next to me, placing her head on my shoulder. "You must eat."

I nodded, placing a gentle kiss on her forehead. "I promise I will," I responded, taking her hand in mine, sharing our agony. The missing babbles of a child haunted the room as I held Ruby tighter, staring at the wall where a crib once was. I felt my shoulder grow damp as she silently cried onto me. "Come on," I said, picking her up. As we both stood we stared at each other longingly. "We need to keep going," I reminded her, linking my arm with hers as we left the room.

"We do," she reassured me.

"How are you feeling?" Alex asked, sitting next to me. I looked up and smiled, lowering the teacup from my lips.

I shrugged. "I've been better," I joked, "but my mind is a bit clearer than before. How is everyone?"

"Grieving. Joseph is in the living room with Ethel, who last I saw was sleeping. How have you and Yuuto been?"

I looked across from me and studied Yuuto, who was "reading" a novel he found on one of the shelves. He flipped the page, pretending to be invested in the story. "Silent. He's reading and I'm thinking. And yourself?"

"I don't know, to be quite frank. I was just pacing about the living room, so I decided to see how things were going here."

"I think I may interview everyone separately and ask them for possible motives. Ruth said she invited everyone she thinks would be capable of murdering her. Therefore everyone has had an unpleasant experience with her at some point in time. Yuuto has already told me his story, so I should listen to the rest. Though I suspect it'll be difficult to get them to talk since they will not want to admit to anything in fear of seeming suspicious."

"What about those on the list?"

"I'll interview them too."

Yuuto looked up from his book and threw it to the side. "Do you think whoever killed Eddie is the same person as Ruth's killer?"

Alex and I shrugged.

"It's most probable, though I can't understand why," I answered.

Alex gasped. "He may have figured it out, or found something the killer didn't want him to see."

Yuuto raised his eyebrows and looked to me, waiting for a reaction. "If that's the case, what do you think he found?" he asked. The room was silent.

"Stuffed, I'll be. Well, do any of you need anything?" Alex said.

I grinned and took her hand in mine, squeezing it gently as I pulled her into an awkward hug. "Alex, you've been absolutely wonderful to all of us, and a splendid help. I cannot thank you enough, so please, rest. Take some time to yourself. You've done more than you had to."

Alex stood, kissing my forehead. Yuuto squirmed in his seat, throwing his legs over one of the arms of the sofa. "I'll head back to the living room, but if you need anything I'm here for you," she reassured, studying my face before leaving. I grinned.

"Is she the next one?" Yuuto mumbled. I turned my head and hummed in confusion. "Next wife. Your next *victim*," he spat the last word jokingly, with a tint of jealousy.

I laughed. "No, I'm quite fine with the one I have now."

"That's most certainly not what you said yesterday, but if you'd like I'll pretend like it was."

I rolled my eyes, still smiling, and got out of the chair, offering my hand to Yuuto. "Come on, there's work to be done."

Chapter Seven:

You Gathered Us Here Today

I picked up the small notepad I had found and looked up to Ethel, my expression dour. "Ethel, how are you feeling today?" I asked.

She forced a smile. "Could be much better, if I may be so bold."

"That's alright. Now, I'm going to ask you a few things, and I need you to be as sincere as possible. Can you do that for me?"

"Walter, you don't have to butter me up. I know why I'm here and what is going to happen. There's no need to sugarcoat it. Ask away," she snapped, fumbling with her clothes. She wore a loose pink blouse tucked into a long, pleated skirt. A large strand of her hair hung over her face, covering her left eye.

"Right, sorry. Ethel, did you ever have any problems with Ruth?"

"No, none at all. I may not have been as close to her as Liza, but we still got along fairly well. She took care of me," she answered.

"Very well. Why do you think she trusted Liza with the key and not you?"

"You said it yourself, she's confident and rarely shows herself unless I consent to it, which makes her good at keeping secrets."

"Yes, but why not you? You're the host and you're quiet. Why did she ask Liza specifically? Why couldn't it be a secret shared among you both?"

"I'm not sure," Ethel responded hesitantly.

"Do you remember Liza receiving the key?" I asked, leaning forward.

Ethel shifted in her seat. "I vaguely remember the meeting, though I wasn't paying much attention."

I nodded. "Whenever you would meet with Ruth, did she ever request to speak to Liza instead?" I questioned, crossing my arms in front of me. I noticed Ethel pressing her lips together, realizing what I was implying.

"I had no problem with Ruth preferring Liza over me. It's not something she did consistently. Though she may not have loved us both equally, I know she loved me still. We're both different people, so she treated us as such. She didn't have to like us both the same."

I looked down at Ethel's hands, noticing her right hand flinch as the left one clutched her skirt.

"Pardon me, Ethel, but I think you don't really believe that," I confessed, watching as her face turned red.

Ethel blinked rapidly before taking a stuttered breath. "I argued with Ruth about it once. I'm well aware Liza is easier to speak to. That's why she exists. However, she wouldn't ever stop talking to Liza, or asking about Liza, and it became irritating. It is a fear you will never fully understand, Walter, not unless you're ever like me."

"What fear is that?"

"The fear of being replaced."

I looked down and offered my hand to her, which she falteringly took. "So it did bother you? Ruth preferring Liza?"

"I'm the host of this body, not Liza. Liza is only a part of it, a part of *me*. But the way Ruth would speak to her or attempt to coax me into switching always made me feel as though Liza would become the host, as if life would be better if I was only a part of Liza, not the other way around." Ethel sniffled as she lowered her head, allowing her hair to fall over her face. I lifted my hand and pushed her hair back, caressing her cheek.

"Liza may be wonderful, but so are you. You're brilliant, fearless, and beautiful. You hold a strength no one in this house will ever acquire, and you must never forget it. I may have only just met you, but trust me when I say that you are one of the most magnificent people I have ever come across, Ethel, I mean it. So, no, life would not be better if Liza was the host, and I'm sorry Ruth ever made you feel that way."

Ethel's eyes teared up as she gripped my hands, her teeth showing as she smiled. "Walter, I won't ever be able to express how happy you've made me. Thank you."

I nodded, squeezing her hand in return. "Before I let you go, could you tell me about the argument with Ruth?"

Ethel sighed. "She kept insisting on speaking to Liza, and I couldn't help myself. I was tired of it, so I yelled at her. The memory is slightly fuzzy, but I remember throwing something in my fury. I immediately stopped and apologized, embarrassed by my improper behavior. Then I left. This was maybe two months ago, and I haven't personally spoken to her since; quite frankly I was surprised to have been invited."

I jotted down a couple of notes before I asked another question. "Looking back, do you think she would have thought you to be capable of murdering her over the situation?"

Ethel's eyes went wide before they immediately relaxed. "No," she replied, shaking her head. I scribbled something down before looking up.

"Did Liza ever have any similar or worse situations with Ruth?"

"Not that I know of. You'd have to speak with her later, but it seemed they got along fabulously. She even called to apologize last week."

I hugged her before allowing her to leave, asking her to bring in Joseph.

"Good morning." She yawned, sitting in front of me. *"Did you sleep well? It sounded like you did,"* She teased,

raising an eyebrow as She smirked. "I almost thought I would be lucky enough not to see your face today," I joked, smiling. She snorted and began pacing the room. *"How sweet of you. Do you plan on talking to Yuuto the same way?"* She remarked, stopping by the window as she looked out. My shoulders tensed. "I don't know what you're implying, but I'd like you to stop," I muttered.

She snickered, looking back to me. *"Walter, if you didn't want me to say anything, you know very well I wouldn't have."*

Joseph knocked on the door before entering, smiling. I looked to my right and noticed She was gone, sighing as I motioned Joseph to take a seat. "How may I help you?" Joseph asked.

"I have a few questions. That's all. I need you to be as honest as you can be."

Joseph nodded.

"Did you ever have any problems with Ruth?"

Joseph gripped her hands, inhaling suddenly as she straightened her back. "Yes, I did. Though it wasn't with me personally."

I nodded, pulling out my notepad as I got ready to jot down her statement. "What happened?"

Joseph looked out the window before looking back. "Ruth was having an affair with a married man for a long time. She told me about it." Joseph lifted her lips quickly, looking at the ground as if watching a memory unfold. "I love Ruth dearly, but what she did was simply unacceptable, and beyond sinful. I was disappointed in her." Joseph looked up to me and shifted her head. "I've always believed that God has a reason for everything, but I could and still cannot find a reason for what Ruth did. I can only hope God has forgiven her for her sins."

"Did you expect to be invited to this party?" I asked.

"Quite honestly, no," She stated, furrowing her brows. "Why, is that important?"

I stood up and offered to walk her back, my mind whirring with theories. As we made our way into the library, I asked everyone to take a seat before speaking. "After speaking to you all individually I have come to notice many things, but something I found intriguing was that all of you were surprised to be invited to her party,

126

and all of you have had problems with her in the past. Have any of you truly forgiven her for whatever she did to you?"

The room was quiet as everyone looked around, waiting for a reply, but no one spoke. I smiled. "She invited the people she believed were most likely to kill her after receiving a death threat. All of you have a motive to kill her, and just as she guessed, one of you did." I paused, studying the faces around the room. "Is there anyone who would like to confess to anything before I continue the investigation?"

"Does that mean that everyone you interrogated was not on the list?" Ethel asked, raising her hand halfway.

I grinned. "I made sure to interview everyone, Ethel, which is why it makes my findings even more surprising. Even those who were on the list had some sort of unforgivable dispute with her." I paused. "Anything else?"

"What about Eddie?" Joseph asked, gripping her hands together.

"I have my ideas as to what happened to Eddie, though if you have any theories, Joseph, I suggest you share them now," I said. Joseph gulped before looking to Yuuto.

"I don't mean to pry, but Eddie and Yuuto didn't seem to be on good terms last night."

Yuuto slammed his fist against the arm of his chair before springing to his feet. "Joseph, you seem quite keen on pointing fingers and making accusations, are you sure there's nothing you'd like to share with the rest of the group? Possibly a sin you'd like to confess too? Wouldn't want you to ask God for forgiveness behind bars, *darling*." Yuuto spat the last word poisonously.

Joseph gasped, waiting for someone to speak up in her defense. The room remained silent.

I stepped forward, quickly glancing at Yuuto. "Enough. I'm going to examine Alton's body. I'll return momentarily."

"Would you like for me to come?" Alex asked.

I shook my head. "No, Yuuto can assist me," I answered, causing Yuuto to whip his head toward me in surprise.

"You want my help?" he whispered, his head held high. I tried not to smile as I held out my hand.

"It's what you wanted, isn't it?" I reminded him. "Come on, let's get going. Alex, no one leaves this room."

"Walter, you have to eat," Ruby cooed, pushing the plate closer to me. I felt my arms grow numb as she gently touched them. "Starving yourself won't make things any easier, neither will sickness or death."

I looked up to her, cupping her chin. "Do you hate me, Ruby?" I choked. She sighed as she picked up her plate.

"I could never hate you, Walter, not even now," she answered sincerely, making her way into the kitchen.

"Ruby, I'm leaving," I reminded her, tears forming in my eyes. Ruby gulped before turning to face me.

"I know, Walter. And it's best if you do, for your own sake. You're making yourself suffer by staying here."

I looked down at the plate of food in front of me, crossing my arms. "I'd rather you hate me, Ruby, than be so understanding."

Ruby half smiled as she placed the plate on the sink, returning to the dining table. "We both do, Walter. But it is

what it is. We have to move on from this, and if going to Ruth
will help you, then so be it. I'll figure something out."

"You won't be able to get a proper job. And you need
someone with you, some company; you're sharing the same
dreadful pain as I, possibly worse," I cried.

She shrugged. "Walter, I'll be alright. As I said, I'll
figure something out."

"You're brilliant. You can accomplish so much," I
mumbled, sniffling.

Ruby reached over and held my cheeks before planting a
kiss on my forehead. "And so can you, my love."

"We need to keep going, the both of us," I whispered,
repeating our mantra to her. "We need to keep going."

Ruby's eyes began to water as she fully smiled for the
first time in months. "And you will."

I held Yuuto's hand as we took a deep breath. "Are
you sure you want to go in?" I asked softly, looking to
Yuuto. He nodded.

"I want to help you," he stated, tightening his grip
on my hand. "Come on, we need to keep going."

I froze at the words, staring at Yuuto as he pulled at me to follow him. "Walter, what's wrong?" he asked, tugging at my hand again.

"Sorry, that's something someone I knew used to say." I shivered, forcing a smile as we entered the kitchen. *"Reminiscing, darling?"* She smirked. I whipped my head around, inhaling sharply. I slammed the kitchen door shut behind me, making it clear I didn't want her around. I tiptoed over to Eddie's corpse, where Yuuto struggled to remain composed. "You don't have to be here," I told Yuuto.

"Damn it, Walter, make up your mind. Do you want me here or not?" Yuuto spat nervously.

I swallowed. "I just want to make sure you're okay."

Yuuto nodded, taking a shaky breath. He moved aside in order to allow me to examine Eddie. I knelt down next to him, closing his eyes. I looked down to his stab wound, picking up the knife from his hands. I looked it over before turning to Yuuto. "Do you mind holding this for a minute?" I asked. Yuuto took a deep breath before nodding and reaching his hand out. I shifted and took a better look at the wound, my lips forming a straight line as my eyebrows pulled together. I looked down at his wrists, noticing a cut on his right hand. "He struggled, tried to grab the knife from his attacker's hand," I noted aloud.

"Walter, darling, you might want to look at this," Yuuto whispered, patting my shoulder. I turned around and watched as he lowered the knife. "There's dried blood that's close to the handle."

"Did you touch it?" I asked with concern.

"Heavens no! It simply looks darker, see? I was examining it."

I nodded gratefully and took the knife from his hands, standing. Yuuto washed his hands, lifting the sleeves of his dress shirt to his elbows. I looked away as I felt my face grow warm.

"I think this knife is the same one that killed Ruth; the dried blood implies it was used for a deeper wound," I suspected, turning the weapon in my hands.

Yuuto nodded in agreement, drying his hands with a cloth. "What I'm wondering, however, is how Eddie found it."

I looked around him, cracking my knuckles as I knelt down at Eddie's feet. "Obviously outside, he's wearing his trench coat. Though I wonder what made him go outside in the first place. Was anyone down here with him?"

"I don't know, though I suppose Alex let him come down, so you'd have to ask her."

I nodded, annoyed he was able to go outside by himself. *"They all knew not to be alone; you mentioned it multiple times. It's his fault he's dead."* I sighed, ignoring Her statement. "His shoes are muddy, meaning he walked on dirt. It hasn't rained, so he might have gone out to water the plants." I picked up his right hand, looking at his fingers. "There's dirt under his nails, so that confirms he was gardening. Why so early in the morning?"

"He was making a quiche," Yuuto said, pointing at the vegetables set next to the stove. "Ruth grows her own herbs, fruits, and vegetables, so I assume he went out to get some ingredients."

I scratched my head, standing next to Yuuto. "I still don't understand, how did Alton find the murder weapon?"

"Stumbled upon it by luck?" Yuuto suggested.

I sighed. "Not lucky for him. I'll check to see if there's anything else here, but I think we should bury him soon. It wouldn't be right for there to be two corpses sprawled on the ground around the house."

Yuuto nodded and pushed back his short hair, letting it slip through his fingers. "Should we wear black?" he asked, shifting his weight from left to right.

"If you deem it appropriate. Joseph could even say a few things in Alton's honor." Yuuto smiled at my suggestion, looking at Eddie. I examined his body once more before placing his arms over his chest, holding onto Yuuto as we left the kitchen. "Will you help me move his body outside?" I asked, walking out into the main entrance. Before he could respond, the phone rang.

Yuuto ran into the dining room and picked it up. "Hello, Ruth's residency. No, I'm afraid she is not available at the moment. May I ask who is speaking?" There was a pause. "I see. Would you like to speak to him?" Another pause. "Of course, I'll fetch him for you." Yuuto pulled the phone away from his ear. "Walter, it's your wife," he whispered, waving the phone out in annoyance. I strolled over and took it from his hands, briefly brushing his fingers with mine.

"Walter, where are you? Is everything alright?" Helen asked worriedly.

"Everything is perfectly fine, my love. Don't worry. I was meaning to call you, but I lost track of time. I'll be spending the rest of the day with Ruth in order to catch up, and tomorrow we can go out into town and explore before heading back to England. How does that sound?" There was silence on the other end.

"I assume you haven't heard the news then," Helen sighed.

I turned to face Yuuto, frowning. "What happened?"

"London is in a complete blackout. It's absolute chaos. Everyone was told to cover their doors and windows with black paint after receiving a bomb threat from Germany. We can't go back now, it's far too dangerous."

My heart dropped. I reached out my free hand to Yuuto, motioning for him to hold it. Yuuto stood next to me, intertwining his fingers with mine as he placed his head on my shoulder in worry. "When did the blackout occur?"

"My love, it's *occurring*. Yesterday was when the order was issued, before sundown. Tonight the same thing will happen. It's terrible," Helen informed me.

My breath hitched as my grip tightened around Yuuto's hand. "Then I suppose we'll have to stay for a while longer. When will the blackout end?"

"No one knows, though there's a rumor England will take part in the war."

I gasped, looking over to Yuuto. "By God! Thank you, Helen, I was entirely clueless. I'll return to Ruth now, though I should be back tonight. We can make plans then. Take your mind off of things as best as you can, and leave the worrying to me."

"Do you think England will be alright?"

"I don't know, Helen, but I hope so," I choked at my final words.

"I'll see you tonight then. Give my love to Ruth for me; and a million apologies for intruding last night. Cheerio."

"I'll see you soon," I said, hanging up. I slumped onto Yuuto, sighing deeply.

Yuuto looked up to me. "What's wrong?"

"I've been living here for the past two or three months, and I was planning to return to England tomorrow. Though it appears Germany differs with my plans, so I must stay here longer. London is in a blackout in order to hide from the bombs," I explained, to which Yuuto gasped, lifting his hands to his lips as he pulled away from me. "Helen believes England will take part in the war soon."

Yuuto shook his head in disbelief. "That's absolutely horrendous, Walter. I'm sorry."

I shrugged. "England may soon be at war, and my best friend is dead. I'm afraid sympathy will do nothing to solve either issue, so I'd rather not receive any. Come on, Yuuto, we need to keep going."

We made our way to the library where the rest of the group waited. Alex quickly stood, asking if we had found anything. "Alton went outside to get ingredients for this morning's breakfast until he stumbled upon the murder weapon. When he brought it back inside, his killer was waiting and took the weapon from him, stabbing him with it and making it seem like a suicide," I hypothesized. "None of this is guaranteed; however, Yuuto and I found convincing evidence that directed me to this conclusion. Does anyone have any questions?"

The group looked at each other, waiting for someone to speak up. "What will happen to Eddie?" Ethel shivered as she placed her head on Joseph's shoulders, who wrapped her into a hug.

"We'd like to properly bury Alton outside, though we were hoping Joseph could say a few words beforehand as a kind of farewell."

Joseph looked up, her eyes tearing up. "I can try, though I'd rather not speak for long. It's too painful."

"I'll say a few words," Yuuto offered.

I took his hand in mine, caressing his arm. "Are you sure?" I asked cautiously.

Yuuto nodded.

Yuuto and I moved Eddie's body outside while Alex began to shovel a hole. Ethel and Joseph waited by Alex, unable to help due to their attire.

"Yuuto, come give me a hand, won't you? It'll take too long if I do this by myself," Alex said. Yuuto nodded and pulled a shovel out of the shed, digging with Alex.

The lawn was large, with flowers scattered around the grass. Under the living room window was a small garden of berries and vegetables. I looked at Alex, who threw her shovel over the hole and picked up her baggy pants, which were meant to be worn by a male. As the group surrounded the large hole, Yuuto and I lifted Eddie's body and slowly lowered it to the ground. My stomach churned as I stepped aside, looking down at a silent Eddie, one which would never move or cook again. "We are gathered here today to celebrate the life of Edward Lee Alton, who has now returned to his home with Our God, the Father," she began, fumbling with the skirts of her long dress. "I would like to share a reading."

"As you wish, Father." I nodded.

Joseph stood straight and cleared her throat. "Many of those who sleep in the dust of the earth shall awake; some to everlasting life, others to reproach and everlasting disgrace. But those with insight shall shine brightly like the splendor of the firmament, and those who

lead the many to justice shall be like the stars forever."
After a moment of silence, Joseph lifted her chin and
pointed to Yuuto. He stepped forward and looked at each
individual before quickly glancing at the ground.

"Edward Lee Alton was a good man, one whose
life did not deserve to come to such a devastating end.
Though he had many flaws and faults, as do we, so I pray
he's been forgiven and his killer is brought to justice."
Yuuto's voice wavered as he took a shaky breath. "He was
a lover to some, a friend to many, and an inspiration to all;
and despite what most believe, I hold no hatred for this
man and hope where he is now is better than the
unworthy earth he walked on." He looked down to the
ground, clutching his hands together. "Eddie, I never got
to tell you, but I loved you, and I hope you are well."

"Let us go in peace to live out the Word of God."

Chapter Eight:

Living Out the Word of God

I took out the candles one by one, setting them on the ground. "This is taking too long," Alex mumbled from the doorway. It was the first time I had heard her sound exasperated.

"There are a few more candles. I'm going as fast as I can," I responded.

Alex sighed and shook her head. "Not the candle thing, Walter, the case! I don't mean to pressure you, mate, but you're running out of time. We'll be having lunch soon."

I gripped the candle tightly before placing it on the ground again. "If you don't like the speed I'm going at, you can solve the case yourself."

Alex looked into the room, frowning. "I didn't mean to upset you, but you know I'm right. Everyone's beginning to whine."

I raised an eyebrow. "Who is?"

"The likely; Joseph desperately wants to leave, and Ethel's becoming uneasy." Alex stepped further into the room, moving close to me. "Also, your wife called again."

I dropped the candle I had picked up from the closet as my eyes went wide and I stared at her, the glass shattering at my feet. Alex stared at the broken candle.

"What did she say?"

"She wouldn't tell me what she wanted. She wants to speak to you personally."

"Is she coming?"

"I wouldn't be surprised if she did. She sounded quite irritated," Alex responded, shrugging.

I looked down at the candles on the ground, then back at the ones on the shelf. I pushed the pieces of broken glass and wax into a pile with my shoe, and shoved it to the side. "Then we'll get ready for her arrival. I'm positive Ruth's hiding something in here. She wouldn't leave something so suspicious behind and expect me not to look into it. Can you cook?" I asked.

Alex shook her head. "I can't, but Ethel said Liza can."

"Both of you can go down to the kitchen and prepare lunch. Joseph and Yuuto can stay here with me unless Joseph would like to help you both," I stated. Alex agreed and left, leaving me alone surrounded by candles.

After a few minutes, Yuuto and Joseph made their way into the room. "What in the name of life and liberty are you doing, Walter?" Yuuto asked while Joseph picked up one of the candles.

"Lavender's an interesting choice of a candle, isn't it?" Joseph asked, looking up. I turned to face her, ignoring Yuuto's exasperation. "Lavender is said to represent elegance and is at times associated with wealthy women. I'm not sure what it is you're looking for, Walter, but I wouldn't be surprised if this excessive amount of lavender is just Ruth's way of reminding us all of how rich she is."

I shook my head in response. "While your observation is extraordinary, I don't believe that's the message she left behind. Her wealthiness is obvious; there's no need to fill a closet with lavender candles. Besides, why would she show off her wealth to herself through lavender scented candles?"

"I wouldn't put it past her," Yuuto mumbled, walking around the room. Joseph took a seat on Ruth's bed, scanning the odd bedroom.

I dragged out a candle on the far corner, watching as a note floated to the floor from beneath the candle. I dropped to my knees and swept it off the ground, making my way to the writing desk as I began to unfold the note. My darling Walter, I remember the day your daughter was born like it was yesterday.

My breath hitched as I dropped the note onto the desk as my quivering hands shot up to my lips.

"What's wrong?" Joseph asked, her voice slow and cautious.

She was beautiful, with your smile and Ruby's eyes. I wish I could have stayed with you both longer, or kept insisting on you both staying in America. Though your hearts were set in London, and I didn't want to interfere. I was so happy for you, Walter, the joy in your face is one I wish I could see again. Then the terrible day came when you both learned she was ill, and there was nothing that could be done to cure her. The day she died was an unfortunate one, one I wish I could have aided you in. The day you called to ask if you could live with me I told you that you could not, that you should stay with Ruby, even though you were both separated. I lied and said I didn't understand why you would want to leave, but I knew perfectly well. The reason I denied you, Walter, was because I was afraid. I was afraid of having to take care of you while you grieved over a child and a marriage that wasn't ours. I was envious of the life you had made with someone else. I was envious that the cause of your joyful expressions was not me for a very long time, so I refused to take you in when I should have.

I jumped at the feeling of Yuuto's hands on my shoulder. "What did you find?" he whispered. Joseph stood, walking up behind me. I turned around and lifted the note, not wanting them to read it.

I assume you know by now that I was not a good person. I assume you also know that I wasn't as compassionate as you believed, and I wasn't as understanding as you made me seem, though I'd like to believe I did try to fit your image of me as best as possible. However, all it did was force me to pretend to be someone I knew perfectly well I was not. In each of my drawers, I have left terrible secrets of mine, ones which I would like you to know of. My darkest thoughts are now yours to keep, and I hope you keep them well. I love you, Walter Grover, and I wish you the best of luck.

I crumpled the note in my hands and threw it on the ground, anger boiling through my veins. "Joseph, go help Alex and Liza with lunch," I hissed, and without a word, Joseph scuttled out of the room. Yuuto's hands stayed on my shoulders. "Yuuto, you should go too."

"I'm not leaving you alone. What did you find?" he asked softly. My shoulders began to shake as tears slowly escaped my eyelids, swimming past my cheeks and nestling on my chin. My hands tightened as if I were holding a sword, and my legs shook in fury. "Walter?"

"She's of absolutely no help, leaving things like this behind. Leaving her secrets and her problems for me to solve and keep to myself. I can guarantee she enjoyed this. In a deeply disturbing way she enjoyed leaving notes and letters scattered around like some sort of game she expects I'll play. This is murder, *her* murder, but she was so convinced she would be saved she didn't even bother leaving anything with meaning other than a ridiculous list of people she assumes had no motive to kill her, but even some of those have the perfect reason to." I sniffled. "I've been so focused on her past, on trying to comprehend what she was like, I've forgotten why I'm still here. I'm so determined to learn what she was like I've forgotten she's dead, and no matter what I learn about her it won't change the fact that while she was here, while she was *alive*, I didn't know her. It's worthless trying to get to know her, because what's the point of forgiving someone who will never know they were even forgiven?"

"So that you may live on," Yuuto replied. "She may be dead, but you are not. There's nothing she can do to make up for her mistakes, so all we can do is learn to live with what she did and carry on. I don't know what that note said, but whatever it says, remember it's part of the past now, and there's nothing that can be done but to keep going, keep *living*." Yuuto turned me around, wiping the tears from my face.

"I'm afraid I won't ever find out who killed her. I'm afraid I was never good enough to save her."

Yuuto wrapped his arms around me, resting his chin on my shoulder. "Walter, I may have only just met you, but I can promise you that though you may not be a hero or a savior, you are far more than good enough, and I wouldn't mind spending the rest of my life proving it to you," he assured me, pulling away to study my eyes.

As my heart began to race under his gaze, I lifted both of my hands to the sides of his face and without hesitation, closed my eyes and drew him into a kiss.

I held my breath as he placed his hands on my neck, deepening the kiss. My hands shook as a warmth overcame me, and I backed away in order to catch my breath. "I'm sorry, I should have—" my apology was quickly cut off as Yuuto grinned and tugged my shoulders, kissing me again. I tried not to smile as I dug my fingers into his hair, furrowing my brows as the kiss deepened. It wasn't until we heard a knock on the door that I realized how desperately I wanted to stay there with him, and never think about anything else.

"Walter?" Alex asked from the door. Yuuto traced my lips with his forefinger as he placed his forehead on mine, smiling.

"Yes?" I called out hoarsely. Yuuto snorted.

"Your wife has arrived."

"You should tell her," Alex had advised. Though doing so proved to be harder than she made it out to be.

I shifted in my seat, debating a way to begin the conversation. "Helen—"

"My love, I trust you immensely and I understand you haven't seen Ruth in a very long time. However, I told you that our country, our *home*, is under fire, and you did nothing. I'll say it again: I trust you, but I'm also not an idiot. What's going on?" Helen interrupted.

I took a deep breath before telling her of last night's events, filling her in on both Ruth's and Eddie's murders. Helen's eyes widened, slumping in her seat as I spoke. Once I was done, I sat silently and waited for her reaction.

"Do you know who the killer is?" she whispered, leaning forward. We sat in the dining room while the rest of the group waited in the library.

"I have my theories, but, no, I don't," I stated disappointedly. "Though that's what I've been trying to figure out."

Helen sighed before sitting properly on her seat, rubbing the sides of her head. "Who do you know you can trust?" I told her about the list Ruth left behind. "Are you certain you can trust them?"

"I know I can trust Alex for certain, but some of the people on the list also have a strong motive to have killed her, so she could have been wrong," I informed her.

Helen nodded. "Why didn't you tell me?" she asked.

I shrugged. "I didn't want to worry you or get you involved. For Christ's sake, Ruth made it clear she doesn't even want the police to know about what's happening."

After a moment of silence, Helen stood, patting the skirt of her dress. "Well, I'm sure there are still things you haven't informed me about, but there's no time to worry about that. How can I help?"

I blinked rapidly, confused by her question. "Help? You want to help?" I asked. *"Ooh, I like her. Why can't she always be like this?"* I heard Her whistle from behind me.

"You can get more work done with my help. I may not be a detective, but neither is Alex. There must be something I can do." Helen stretched out her hand to me, waiting for me to hold it. I shivered before taking it. "I promised you I would do anything to prove I am a worthy wife, and if assisting you in solving a murder will do so, then so be it."

My eyebrows furrowed as I stared at her, still holding onto her hand. Just then Yuuto walked in, and my hand quickly pulled away. "Yuuto, is something wrong?" I asked.

Yuuto stared at Helen, his jaw gradually dropping as he realized who she was. *"Well, hello, you must be the infamous Helen."* He grinned, making his way to her. I jumped to my feet and watched as he lifted her hand to his lips, glancing to me as he kissed it. "I'm terribly sorry if I interrupted anything, but Alex would like to know how much longer you are going to take since we're all dying to eat something."

I took a deep breath before forcing a smile, pulling Helen aside. "We were just about done with our conversation, so if she's ready, then we may eat lunch."

"Perfect. She asked for you to tell her yourself. Apparently she has something else she'd like to talk to you about."

"Very well. Are you coming with me?" I asked.

Yuuto grinned, walking over to one of the chairs and sitting, placing his feet on the table before winking at me. "I'll wait here with Helen if you don't mind. Do you?" he teased. I chuckled before shaking my head, forcing a smile as I steadied my breathing.

"Not at all. I'll return with the others," I said slowly, eyeing him before walking over to Helen and kissing her cheek. "Behave," I warned Yuuto while I stepped out of the room.

Once the doors were closed, I turned around and pressed my ear against a crack, listening intently for any conversation. After a few minutes, I heard Yuuto's feet fall back to the ground.

"So you're Yuuto?" Helen asked. I assumed her arms were crossed as she spoke, something she did whenever she met new people in an uncomfortable environment.

"The one and only. How have you been enjoying America? I've been told you and Walter live in England."

"We do, and it's been pleasant. Not much to do around this area, but it's very different from London. Sometimes it feels as though all there is in this world is mountains and endless trees," she joked, earning a laugh from Yuuto.

"But isn't it nice? I can't help but look at the hills or the lake and simply feel blessed to be where I am. After years of being surrounded by bad company and peculiar smells, the sunny skies and the grassy hills are truly a sight for sore eyes. It's impossible to take for granted."

I smiled at his words.

"It sounds like from what you've said you haven't lived a good life."

"You couldn't possibly have been friends with Ruth and lived a good, fair life," Yuuto replied.

"Were you close with her?" Helen asked. There was silence. "Closer than the others?"

"If you're trying to interrogate me, I'll let you know it's not necessary. Your . . . *husband* has already done so."

I rolled my eyes at the jealousy dripping off of his tongue as he spoke.

"I apologize, I'm just trying to be helpful to him somehow. Has he spoken to everyone?"

"Yes, at least once. Walter is an extraordinarily brilliant man. You must be very proud of him."

"What else do you think of him?" she asked.

My heart dropped.

"Excuse me?"

"You've only known him for a day, and you seem to think very highly of him. I assume there's a reason for it." There was a pause. "I'm sorry, that was rude."

"It's alright. He's been handling the case well, even though it's someone he loved dearly. He holds no judgment in his heart and is moving this case along quickly, considering the fact that he's doing this by himself for the most part."

I backed away from the door and hurried down to the library, my face heating at Yuuto's words. Once I arrived at the library, I informed everyone that lunch could be served, and allowed them to move to the dining room. As Liza and Joseph walked out of the library, Alex grabbed my hand and pulled me aside, making sure they were both a good distance away. "Alex, what's wrong?"

Alex looked over my shoulder once more before moving her face close to my ear.

"I think I know who the killer is."

I sat at the end of the table, Helen on my left and Yuuto on my right. Liza sat next to Yuuto, and Joseph across from her. Finally, Alex sat at the other end of the table. "This tastes delicious," I complimented, taking another bite of the salad.

"Nothing as good as what Eddie could make, but thank you." Liza smiled. Alex looked over to her, nodding.

Helen placed her fork on the empty plate and looked to Yuuto, then me. "Walter has given me a brief description of all of you, but I'm interested to know more."

Liza lifted her hand, waving. "I'm Liza, Ethel's 'friend,' so to say. She's the host of this body, but currently, I am present."

"You alternate between yourself and Ethel, correct?" Helen asked.

Liza nodded.

"That's amazing. Do you have a job?" Helen asked.

"I'm a secretary."

Helen briefly spoke with everyone around the table, listening to their stories and mentally writing them out. "Helen's a writer," I interrupted eventually, to which Helen blushed.

Yuuto leaned forward, placing his chin on his left hand. "A writer? What do you write?"

"Short stories, though none have been published. Walter says I'm gifted, but I beg to differ."

"Helen, your work is beautiful and poetic. If only you tried, I guarantee you'd be published in minutes. Her stories are almost Shakespearean, due to the twists and meanings she hides in her tales. Every time I reread any I always find something new. It's remarkable," I bragged, leaning forward to kiss her forehead. I noticed Yuuto straightening his posture from the corner of my eye. Helen beamed with pride as I sat back in my seat.

Once everyone was done eating, I asked Liza to speak with me privately, ordering the rest to wait in the library. "I'll come with you," Helen offered.

"You can wait if you'd like—"

"Let me help you," she insisted, taking my hand. "Please."

"We'll have to walk through the ballroom."

"So?"

"Ruth is still in there," I whispered. Helen looked down at her feet then back to me.

"I'll close my eyes. I keep forgetting Alex isn't Ruth." She laughed softly, trying to lighten the mood. I took her hand as we left the dining room and gradually made our way into the ballroom. Liza opened the doors, holding them open for Helen and me to enter. She dug her face into my arm, shivering as we walked past her corpse. "Are we close to her?" she whispered.

"No," I lied, looking over Ruth's body before quickly shoving Helen into the living room. "It's alright now, you can open your eyes."

Liza and I sat across from each other while Helen stood behind me, looking around the room every so often.

"How can I be of service to you?" Liza asked, smiling.

"Your name was on the list," I bluntly stated though she remained unphased. "Do you know why?"

Liza nodded. "She trusted me and loved me just as I loved her. Besides, I have no reason to hate her."

"I beg to differ," I countered.

Liza raised an eyebrow. "What makes you think so?"

157

"She played favorites according to Ethel; in fact, she and Ethel had quite a fight over it once. You told me before all you want to do is protect and care for Ethel, so I'm sure once you realized how upset Ethel was, you no longer loved Ruth as much as you claim. Am I wrong?"

Liza sat quietly, crossing her legs and looking up to Helen before smiling. "I'd be lying if I said you were."

I nodded, looking over Liza. I noticed how she sat up confidently and unshaken, unlike Ethel, who slumped and crossed her legs in anxiousness.

"Do you remember the fight between Ethel and Ruth?"

Liza shook her head. "I'm afraid I don't remember it. I wasn't really there."

"I think you were. I also think you were the one who let Alton outside."

Liza shifted uncomfortably in her seat, furrowing her brows. "Sorry? What are you implying?"

"Ethel told me her memory of the argument between her and Ruth was blurry, meaning she wasn't fully present in the moment; you had to be. Alex also informed me that you took Alton out of his room, and

Alex allowed it since she knows your name is on the list. Isn't it interesting that the one time nor Alex or I am in a room, someone dies? You knew Ruth trusted you. She even gave you the key to her secret room, so no one would suspect you. Not only that, but you could hide within Ethel, the perfect cover." I briefly paused.

Liza's face turned red as she shook her head, gripping her skirts. "I asked Alton if he could make breakfast and offered to help. I'm good with cooking. We went downstairs and talked for a bit. Then he said he didn't want my help, and I went back upstairs. And during Ruth's murder I was in the restroom. Joseph saw me."

"She saw Ethel enter the restroom, but nobody saw you leave. You could have gone in, switched, and killed Ruth. There was also a flower in your hair when Ethel returned to the dining room, and the murder weapon was found outside."

"Ethel got it from the bathroom. She was in there braiding her hair the entire time. We didn't switch, I promise," Liza stated, her breath quickening as she attempted to remain calm.

"I'm terribly sorry, Liza, but your motive is strong and there is enough evidence that criminalizes you. If you confess your crimes, your punishment will not be as severe."

Liza shot up, running to the door. However, Helen immediately grasped Liza's arm before pulling her down. "It wasn't me!" Liza screeched, scratching at Helen. "Let me go. It wasn't me!"

I pushed Helen aside before scooping up Liza from the ground. "Until we can prove otherwise, Liza, you're guilty of Ruth's murder."

"Are you certain?" Helen whispered as I locked the guest room.

"There's much evidence that proves she's the killer," I stated, leading Helen out of the hallway and toward the stairs.

"But you still don't believe she did it, do you? After her outburst, she followed you willingly and seemed almost humiliated once the rest of the group heard your announcement. Besides, you told everyone to stay a while longer, telling me you aren't sure if you believe she's the culprit."

I smiled, shaking my head. "Helen, does anything ever slip past you?" I jokingly asked.

Helen exhaled quickly and giggled, squeezing my hand before walking ahead of me. "No, Walter. Nothing does."

Once Helen and I entered the library, Joseph, Yuuto, and Alex stood patiently at the other end of the room. I noticed almost immediately Yuuto's eyes were glistening. "I'd like to collect more evidence to prove Liza is the murderer. I'm certain Ruth left something behind that could further prove her guiltiness."

"She didn't confess?" Yuuto asked.

"Why would she when she knows there's still hope for her?" Joseph sneered. I slowly turned my head to her, frowning.

"So what now?" Alex sighed.

"You're all free to leave, though I'd appreciate if you'd give me your contact information in case I need any of you for anything."

"Oh, bless the Lord. What will happen to Ruth?" Joseph spoke.

"I'm afraid we can't leave her out for much longer, so I plan on burying her soon. Though I'd like to stick to her last wishes as much as possible and collect enough evidence before finally letting her rest," I answered.

Joseph nodded, picking up the skirts of her dress.

"Well then, I'll be in the restroom. I must change out of these clothes before leaving. Where would you like for me to write my information?" she asked. I told her I'd find a notebook and let her leave.

Once Joseph had left the room, Alex turned to me wide-eyed.

"May we stay and help?" Yuuto asked, preventing Alex from saying whatever was on her mind.

"If you'd like, though you don't have to stay here any longer than you need to."

"I'd love to stay and help, but I must get some sleep. I'll gather some paper from upstairs and write down the hotel's information, is that alright?" Alex asked.

Helen offered to go with Alex upstairs, leaving me with Yuuto once more.

Yuuto stood a good distance away for a moment. I noticed him look over my shoulder before slowly approaching me, slipping his hands into mine. "How are you feeling?" he whispered. I shrugged in response. "I hope you realize I'm staying with you."

"Helen's staying too."

"Good, I like her," Yuuto said, smiling. "Though I like you a significant amount more."

I grinned, shaking my head. "Yuuto . . ."

"I know. You have a wife who clearly loves you, and you kissed me out of impulse. I know it didn't mean anything, it's alright," he said, forcing a smile as he lowered his head.

I picked up his chin and touched his cheeks, shaking my head as my smile dropped. "You're mistaken, Yuuto. That kiss certainly meant something to me, more than you could ever comprehend. However, as you said, I have a wife. Though I may not love her in the way she thinks I do, I still care for her greatly, and being with you at the moment would hurt her a great deal, and I can't allow that. I don't want to cause her pain." I took a shaky breath. "I kissed you because I wanted to, Yuuto, and nothing has felt so right in a very long time. So please understand, I'd love nothing more than to be with you, but I'd like to treat my wife with the respect she deserves," I told him, kissing the right corner of his lips.

"Thank you," Yuuto choked out, chuckling lightly. I smiled at the sound of his laugh, wanting nothing more than to kiss his reddened lips once more.

"You disgusting fathead, how could you?"

Though I'd be lucky if I even got the privilege to look at him again.

Chapter Nine:

The Inevitable Is in Fact, Inevitable

"How are you doing?" Ruth asked.

I shifted the phone closer to my ear. "I've seen better days, to be frank, but I'm in a good place."

"Where are you living now?"

"An apartment a few streets away from where I lived before, still in London."

"Good! And how's Ruby?" Ruth's words were cautious, but gleeful all the same.

I sighed. "I haven't spoken to her since I left, so a week or two ago."

"I see. Poor thing, how did she handle the whole matter?"

I remembered Ruby hugging me before I got on the taxi, how she wished me luck and hoped we'd meet again. She reminded me for the fifth time that morning that all she wanted was for me to be happy since I was all she has left. "She was horrifyingly upset with me, but it was expected. She said she

165

hopes never to see me again," I lied. It seemed much better than the truth.

"Don't forget it was all for the better. By the way, are you able to visit soon? I know you're still getting settled at your new home, but I'd love to see you."

I frowned. "I thought you'd be busy since you weren't able to take me in."

There was brief silence on the other side of the phone. I wondered what she was doing. "I told you, Walter, it's not that I'm busy, but I just think it wouldn't be best for you to stay with me. What if Ruby needs help? I know she doesn't want to see you, but aren't you all she has left?" I grew stiff at her words. Ruth spat out an apology, saying something about how it wasn't in her place to say what she did, but my mind wandered to the memory of Ruby. "Walter? Are you still there?"

"Yes, I am, sorry. I must head out, still need to unpack. I'll call you later."

"No, wait, before you go could you say something nice?"
I hung up the phone.

Tears began to boil behind my eyelids, threatening to pour out. I gritted my teeth as I growled at myself, "Ruby deserved better, Jasmine deserved better . . ." tugging my hair. I

threw whatever objects were in my way to the side as I pulled out
a knife, my hands shaking as I lifted it to my chest. "This is your
fault, Walter. You're hurting everyone," I whispered to myself. I
took what I thought would be my last breath as I raised the knife
in front of me, ready to plunge it into my already lifeless body —

But She appeared, in a way I had never seen her before.
As if She was there, but She truly wasn't. Then, She did what
She did best.

"Don't do it," She whispered.

My savior and my punisher, keeping me alive while
reminding me what it was that made me want to die in the first
place.

I dropped the knife, and that was that.

Joseph stood by the door with her eyes wide, her
hands shaking. She wore a long, buttoned jacket with
black pants and carried a bag which most likely contained
her dress, wig, and such. She didn't look at all like herself.
"How could you do this to Helen?"

Yuuto backed away from me and raised his hands,
shaking his head. "Joseph, it's not what it seems. This is
my fault. I was flirting and he was telling me to stop."

Joseph tightened her lips, shaking her head furiously. "Lying is a sin, Yuuto, and for this, you shall go straight to Hell! Do you hear me? To Hell!" she growled. I moved in front of Yuuto, wrapping my arms protectively around him.

"Joseph, please calm down. I would never do anything that would hurt Helen. I love her. Please understand."

Joseph sniffled as she looked to the ground. "You all say you love each other without truly understanding the power of the word. Forgive me for my reaction, but do not forget that you are a married man, and whether or not you love her, you shall respect and cherish her. I'll take my leave now, but know you've been warned. Love her, Walter, as though you mean it. Even if you don't. She deserves at least to be respected."

"Give your information to Alex," I responded, ignoring her and looking away as she walked out of the room.

Once she was gone, Yuuto sighed in relief, hugging me from behind. "That was absolutely terrifying, Walter."

"Yes, it was. We need to be careful, and by we, I mean you."

Yuuto snorted.

"Come along, we should make sure Joseph actually left her details behind."

I hugged Alex tightly in front of her taxi, slightly bitter she was leaving. "I could never thank you enough. You're absolutely wonderful, Alex, and I do hope I can see you before you leave. I'd love to do something nice for you."

Alex giggled, pulling away. "I'll hold you to it, Walter. I'm glad I was able to help you." Alex moved to Yuuto, shaking his hand before drawing him into a hug. "And, you, don't do anything foolish, alright?" she joked. Yuuto laughed, his eyes glimmering.

"I forgot to tell you how beautiful your hair is. I hope you always leave it long like that. It's gorgeous," Yuuto stated, receiving a blush from Alex.

"Thank you, Yuuto, I will." Finally, she stepped before Helen, chuckling. "I'm sorry I made you think I was

Ruth, truly. I hope I'll be able to make it up to you somehow."

Helen nodded, hugging her momentarily. "Don't stress over it. You did it for a valid reason. I'll be seeing you later on, yes?"

"Too right! I'll see you all before I leave for Australia, yeah? Though it's awful I met you all in these circumstances, I'm glad we met at all. Cheerio!" She looked up to the guestroom in which Liza was being held and smiled ever so slightly, getting into the cab with a sigh. She waved from the car window as she pulled away from the driveway, and we waved back until she was out of sight.

"Joseph left already then?" Helen asked.

I nodded. I took a deep breath before patting Yuuto's back. "Right, then. We have work to do. We need to look through Ruth's belongings and see if we can find any evidence in there."

"You mentioned her not knowing who killed her, so what would make you think she wrote anything that could place Liza as the killer? Wouldn't she know?" Helen asked.

"She may have written something that criminalizes Liza without realizing that it would matter later on. Walter mentioned there was a fight some time ago. She may have written details on it somewhere," Yuuto offered, walking back into the house. I nodded in agreement and followed, grabbing Helen's hand and leading her inside with me.

Once we had made it to Ruth's room, I told Helen to search in the drawers and asked Yuuto to review the notes we had found the night before. I opened a drawer on the side of the writing desk, grabbed a handful of notes, and sighed exasperatedly.

"Why didn't she just get a diary?" Helen asked, sorting through the papers in her hand.

"A diary would be too dangerous. All of her thoughts could be found in chronological order and in one place. She had to hide her identity, so to protect it and stay sane she had to spread out the notes around the room so that no one would find everything she had to say at once," I theorized.

As we skimmed through Ruth's writing, we formed two piles: useless thoughts, and evidence. Just as Yuuto was about to throw a paper onto the "useless" pile,

Helen grabbed his hand, looking to me. "Wait, Walter, stop. Who's Ruby?"

My heart dropped immediately as I looked up to Helen, freezing in my place. Yuuto looked to me worriedly, unsure if he should move. *"There's no hiding it now, Walter. She obviously knows who I am, she just wants reassurance. Are you going to tell her?"* She tormented, looming from behind Helen. I stared at Her as I spoke. "What does it say about her?"

"Ruby rang Ruth, apparently she knew who Ruth really was. Ruth got into some trouble with a friend of hers it seems, and Ruby found out and phoned Ruth to tell her she must speak to you and tell you the truth. Now, who's Ruby?"

I blinked rapidly, shaking my head in confusion. Why hadn't Ruby told me? *"It's not my story to tell. Think of everything you've just learned about Ruth. Would you really believe any of it if anyone other than Ruth had told you?"* I looked down, knowing She was right. "I was married for five years. I moved to London because she didn't want to stay in the States any longer."

"What happened to her?" Helen whispered. Yuuto slowly placed the paper in his hand on its corresponding pile and shifted away, Helen's hand releasing him.

"I'm not sure, but I had to leave her," I spoke shakily.

Yuuto lifted his head, confused at my statement.

"She hated me for it, but there was no other way. I had to go." I noticed Her step away and stand behind Yuuto. *"I did not. Tell them the truth. It's about time someone knows I'm not the crab you make me out to be,"* She insisted, Her lips lifting slowly as She coaxed me. "No, she didn't hate me. She loved me more than anything and agreed it was best that I left, for both of our sakes. I wish she hated me. Even now I wish she wasn't as understanding as she was that day. She knew I had to go, and she let me, even though it meant she would have to struggle to build a new life."

Helen blinked as she processed my words, showing no emotion other than confusion. "Why didn't you tell me?"

"It's not something I like to remember."

"Why did you *have* to leave?" Helen growled, looking down while her eyes began to be outlined with tears.

I gulped, shivering at the memories. I pressed my fingers together, fumbling. "Because I did."

"*Why?*" Helen hissed, glaring at me with disappointment.

There's always something horribly unsatisfying about disappointment. The way Helen's body turned inward as she attempted to control her breath, her eyebrows reaching for each other as she stared at me not as her husband but as a stranger, instantly made me regret my past in a way I had forgotten I was able to. "*She thought you were perfect, her prince charming, and you failed her. You're not what she wanted.*" She tsked. I looked up to Her with a pained look, but She immediately turned away. "Helen, I'm sorry, but I don't want to talk about it. Just know it was for a good reason."

"You left a woman on her own when you knew she'd struggle, dropped her like a used diaper!" Helen argued, fuming.

"She agreed it was best for the both of us. She was fine with it," I whispered, shame overflowing my head. I gulped again as if doing so would keep me from drowning in regret and failure, vividly remembering how I stepped into the cab after Ruby had kissed me for the last time, how I had almost taken my own life thinking I could never get better, and how once again I had disappointed the person whose opinion mattered the most.

I felt Yuuto slip his hand into mine, squeezing it before pulling me into a reassuring hug. I muttered a sound of confusion, allowing him to engulf me in a hug. "I don't know why you did what you did, but you care about people. You wouldn't have left Ruby if it would have hurt her." He subtly kissed the back of my ear out of Helen's view, leaving his lips there for a moment before sitting back in his place. Helen stared at him with surprise, gripping her hands together. He picked up a paper and placed it in my hands, insisting I continue with the work at hand. "Let's keep going, okay? This is a matter that can be discussed later. We have a murder to solve."

"Since when are you the commander?" I sniffled, earning a smile from Yuuto.

"Only when you need me to be. Now come on," he responded. I decided to ignore Helen's questioning stares.

"Eddie finally admitted to his affair with Yuuto. Quite frankly, I'm surprised it took him this long. I am, however, far more shocked at the fact that he claimed it was Yuuto's doing, even though I know he's had brief affairs with some of my guests prior to Yuuto. I suppose this makes him special, doesn't it? I decided to feign surprise and have begun to avoid Yuuto, so that Eddie may think I believe him. I'm curious to see where this may lead."

I looked at Yuuto, who was busy looking through notes. I debated calling him over.

"Did you find anything?" Helen asked poisonously, glaring at me as she raised an eyebrow. My face heated as I understood she was jealous.

"An entry about Yuuto," I informed Helen. Yuuto lowered his hands in confusion, taking the note from my hand and reading it through.

He chuckled before handing it back, pretending not to be as affected as I knew he ought to be. "Ruth's a rat," he mumbled simply. I smiled and rubbed his back in an attempt to comfort him temporarily.

"Helen, may I see the one about Ruby?" I asked. She nodded and handed it over. I took a deep breath before reading it.

"Many months ago I got in a dispute with a lady during my stay in Australia. She accused me of sleeping with her husband (I hadn't, I simply flirted), and to make matters short, it did not end well.

What a small world, the woman is close friends with Ruby, who decided to ring me today and tell me to stay away from Walter, not only that but also to admit to him that I'm not (in her words) 'the angel he perceives you to be.' Funny, he thinks of me as an angel? Then an angel I'll be, for him.

I will not call him, I will not tell him anything. I am his angel. I highly doubt Ruby will tell him. He most certainly will not believe her, but if she does say anything I'll be sure she regrets it."

"That's not terrifying at all," I grumbled sarcastically, placing the paper on the useless pile. "How did I never realize it? How did I never notice how odd she was?"

"She hid information from you in an impressive manner. She knew what she was doing was wrong, everything she stood for was horrid, and she needed someone to tell her she wasn't a bad person. She didn't care if any of us realized what she was really like. She only sought your approval. And to do so, she had to lie at an exaggerated level."

"Walter, say something nice. I don't want you to remember me this way."

I scoffed, shaking my head. "She always used to ask me to tell her something nice," I reminisced. "I never thought much of it. She would say it when we were younger, too."

"How did you meet her?" Helen asked.

I looked down to the papers, shrugging. "When we were about eighteen if I well remember. Met her at an ice cream parlor. She had been attacked by a group of boys, and I gave her my milkshake and company."

"Sounds like you've always been the one to cheer her up," Yuuto noted.

I shrugged. "Simply part of my nature. If I had known then how troublesome she'd be in the future, I don't think I would have been as impressed with her. She was older than me by a year, so I was always fascinated, following her silently. I was one terribly nervous boy." I smiled at the memories. "Anyway, back to the case."

"I met a rather interesting person, Alex. An explorer with a fear of airplanes, bridges, and all sorts of mindless things, yet she has quite a passion for exploration. Not only that, but also she's a retired detective! Used to help a group of officers in their cases, one of which was her brother. She's a brilliant mind, that one. Knowing her could prove very useful in the near future.

That reminds me, Joseph came by today yet again. The brat simply doesn't know when the party's over, does she?"

My eyes went wide at what I read. "I think found something," I stuttered.

"What?" Yuuto asked, his voice suspicious as he read my facial expression.

"She's grown terribly upset over the whole ordeal with her brother-in-law. So what, I made a mistake. It isn't my fault! She came by today telling me it's my fault her sister is in such a depressive state. She says I've ruined her sister's life, but may we not forget an affair takes two. Her brother-in-law is just as guilty of everything as I am."

"Call Joseph," I whispered.

"What?" Helen asked.

I continued to read, my heart racing as I finished the note. "Call Joseph, now!" I exclaimed, waving at Helen. "I need to go get Liza," I realized, jumping to my feet as I sprinted into the hall. I knocked on the door before unlocking it, calling out to Liza, only to find a string of sheets hanging from the window. I looked out curiously, knowing the sheets wouldn't be able to hold her weight. "Liza?" I whispered, confused. Before I could say any more, I noticed someone move from behind me. I turned to face Liza just as she raised a vase above my head.

"I'm so sorry, Walter," she spat, just as I became unconscious.

Sharp pain from the back of my head jerked me awake, causing me to moan out in pain.

"Walter! Oh, thank God!" Yuuto exclaimed, jumping to his feet as he raced to my side and placed his hand on my forehead.

I looked around but noticed everything around Yuuto was blurry.

"How's your head?"

I opened my mouth in order to respond, but only managed a small, painful groan. Yuuto smiled and moved to kiss me, but jerked back and bit his lip once he remembered there were others in the room. He instead squeezed my hand in relief. "Ethel, get Helen. Do you think you can manage that without knocking someone out?" he hissed but received no verbal response. I lifted my right hand and kneaded my head, groaning once more. Yuuto smiled and pulled my hand away, stroking the side of my face. "Don't touch it, you'll make it worse. There's a nasty bruise on your face." He chuckled before following with, "But it doesn't make you any less attractive. Speaking of, would you mind if I kiss you?" His voice was barely above a whisper. I smiled before shaking my head.

"Walter! You're awake, thank goodness!" Helen exclaimed.

Yuuto jumped at her voice, inhaling sharply. "Some other time then," he muttered, moving away and forcing a smile. "I was inspecting the bruise. It seems to be worse than before. Did you bring any ice with you by any chance?"

"No, but I'll fetch some now. Ethel, please come back in."

Ethel shuffled into the room, shamefully looking toward me. She sat by the corner of what I realized was the guest room Ethel was being held in. The walls were a light shade of blue, and the chair Ethel sat on seemed far more comfortable than she made it look. "Walter, how are you feeling?" she asked.

I scoffed in response, waving my arms so Yuuto could help me sit properly. "I've felt better. Surprisingly well, considering a vase was just smashed on my head."

"Would you believe me if I told you I didn't mean to hurt you?" she whispered loudly enough for me to hear.

I laughed. "I most certainly would not."

"Liza didn't want you to become completely unconscious. We thought she killed you. The vase was small enough and she thought it would be enough to daze you while we tried to run out. I can't stay here any longer. We must leave."

"Leave? Why?"

Ethel stared at me nervously. "I can't say, but I must go. Know it's of great importance."

"If so then you should tell me; otherwise I think you're a murderer on the run."

Ethel fumbled with her dress as she looked around thoughtfully. "I have to complete a favor."

It was Yuuto's turn to scoff. "A favor so important you almost killed a man? Ethel, you're supposed to convince us you're innocent."

"I have to send a letter on Ruth's behalf. Well, Liza does, but she doesn't want to show herself, not after what happened with Walter."

"Give me the letter," I ordered.

Ethel opened her mouth to argue, but Yuuto glared at her and put out his hand, earning a shiver from the girl.

She guiltily handed over an envelope she had hidden in her bra.

"Even dead Ruth's problematic," Yuuto grumbled, opening the envelope and reading the letter stuffed inside. "My loving Abe, I would like to say that I hope this letter finds you in good health, but that would be ironic, wouldn't it?

Once this letter reaches you, not only will I be dead, but also you may be the only person who truly loves me. I doubt that the friend who gave this to you even likes me anymore.

I would like for you to pretend as if you never met me and nothing ever happened, as if I never existed in the first place.

If you have any questions, reach out to Walter N. Grover. You can ask Eddie for his information if needed.

Farewell, my love. I love you even now."

I reached out for the letter and took it from Yuuto, shaking my head. "She still talked to him, Joseph's brother-in-law. I need her on the phone, *now*." I mumbled angrily. I saw Her enter the room from the corner of my eye. *"Calm down, Walter. Take a second to relax. I don't feel well at all. I think I'm going to pass out,"* She slurred, tripping over Her own feet. She sat Herself at the end of the bed, caressing Her head. I tried to ignore Her.

"Walter, please calm down," Yuuto whispered, taking my hand once more. I took a deep breath and huffed, looking away.

She rolled Her eyes and looked away. *"Of course you listen to him,"* She complained, though She did not seem bothered at all.

"I'll call Joseph for you. Is there anything in particular you want to know?"

"No, I need her here, I need her to come back," I mumbled, my eyes fluttering.

Yuuto rubbed my back and shook his head. "Walter, *please*. You're being ridiculous. Just let us take care of you. And, Ethel, you're very lucky I haven't thrown a vase at *your* face. Can you not see that this man is impossible to deal with even when he's fully functioning?"

I glared at him but didn't argue.

"I'm sorry that took so long. I forgot where the kitchen was." Helen knocked on the door before entering, placing a towel wrapped around some ice on my head before kissing me. I nodded thankfully and sighed, looking down at my knees.

"It doesn't make any sense. Why did Ruth continue to see this man even after she was caught with him? It's clear they took a break from their meetings, but then they got back together. Joseph's sister must be more than aware of what her husband was doing, so why didn't they stop?" I muttered.

"Ruth was terrible. So was he." Yuuto shrugged.

"She may have done terrible things, but she had morals and reason. Don't forget she still took you in when you were at your worst, Yuuto," I argued.

Yuuto didn't respond, looking down at his hands.

"What are you implying?" Helen asked, glancing to Yuuto.

I picked up the ice from my head and set it to the side, frowning. "Joseph clearly loves her sister, so it would make sense that if Ruth and Joseph's brother-in-law were still seeing each other, Joseph would find out as well."

"Not if they were cautious," Yuuto suggested.

Ethel shook her head as she leaned against the wardrobe diagonal from the bed. "Joseph's sister would be paranoid, and if he were gone for long periods of time she would know. It would be much less difficult to figure out where he was going if he did leave the house to see Ruth."

"I don't like where this is going," Helen muttered. "So if we assume Joseph's sister is as bright as you make her out and Ruth is not as clever as you think, there's no way anyone could hide their affair, is there?"

"No, which means they no longer felt guilty, which would obviously upset Joseph's sister," Yuuto continued.

"If she still cared," Helen suggested.

"Maybe not, but clearly Joseph does," I countered.

"Well then. Joseph's sister knows, tells Joseph, then what?" Helen said exasperatedly.

I looked down. "Then Joseph, the overprotective sister, decides to take matters into her own hands." The room went silent as we all understood. Ethel pulled away from the wardrobe and quickly glanced at the rest of the room. Suddenly, I raised my eyebrows as my jaw dropped, remembering. "The letter. We have to find the letter!" I exclaimed, stumbling out of bed and tripping through the hall as I entered the secret room, scanning my surroundings.

"Walter! You're being ridiculous!" Yuuto screamed from behind me. My thoughts raced as I wondered where she would hide the letter. Yuuto ran into the room, watching as I attempted to stand.

"Check under the mattress, look for an envelope!" I gasped, suddenly dropping as my vision momentarily blurred.

"You absolute idiot, you need to rest!" Yuuto exclaimed worriedly, brushing his hand over my face. I smiled and kissed his fingers, standing again.

"I need to solve this case. Help me look under the mattress."

Yuuto helped me remove the mattress from the bed, and sure enough we found an envelope there. I quickly picked it up and sat down, opening it.

"Ruth,

You've done terrible things worthy of deadly consequences.

Prepare to face your demons very soon."

My hand shot up to my lips, rereading the letter. "Yuuto, get the notepad where Joseph wrote down her information." Yuuto jumped to his feet and ran out. I breathed heavily as I waited for him to come back.

"What did you find?" Helen asked, entering the room along with Yuuto and Ethel. I took the paper and compared the letter with the notepad.

"The handwriting is almost identical. Joseph wrote down her information?"

"Yes."

I sighed and set the letter and the notepad down, standing to face the rest of the group. "Then it's settled. Joseph killed Ruth and Eddie."

PART TWO

Chapter Ten:

Your Last Request

I inhaled sharply as I woke up, clutching the bed sheets I had never seen before.

"The princess has awoken. How was your nap?"

I furrowed my eyebrows and looked to Helen, who sat on a loveseat placed underneath a window. "When did I fall asleep?"

"After you settled on Joseph being the killer; you were beyond dazed and passed out. It hasn't been too long," she informed me, standing and moving to the side of the bed. She lifted my chin and examined the growing bruise on my head. I twitched as I felt her thumb gently sweep it. "I've lost count of the number of times Ethel has come in to apologize. She feels horrible, so do forgive her."

"I have. She acted out of fear, that's all," I assured her.

Helen smiled. "Sometimes I'm convinced you're too good for this world, Walter. A beam of light in a world filled with darkness," she stated, leaving my side and allowing me to slip out of bed.

"You're making me seem like an angel."

"Aren't you?"

I hesitated before deciding on a response. "No. I'm not," I answered softly.

Helen frowned, watching as I stretched and shuffled out of the room.

"They're downstairs if you're wondering. In the dining room!" Helen called out behind me.

Once I had reached the dining room, I looked in and noticed Yuuto standing by the kitchen doors as Ethel chatted with him peacefully. When Yuuto realized my presence, he instantly stood to greet me with a hug.

"You're feeling better, aren't you?" he said close to my ear. I smiled and embraced him, breathing him in as I nuzzled closer to his neck. He giggled in response, holding me tighter. I looked over Yuuto's shoulder and noticed Ethel tapping the table nervously, her eyes darting from me to her hands. I pulled away from Yuuto and scratched my head as I approached Ethel.

"All is forgiven, don't worry," I uttered, extending my hand in order for her to shake it.

She looked at me hesitantly before offering a small smile and taking my hand, shaking it briefly. "Thank you," she said softly.

I nodded in response.

"Walter, I'd like to speak with you for a moment. May I?" Yuuto asked. I nodded and followed him out of the dining room. He pulled me into the library, shutting the door promptly behind me. "I'm very happy you're awake and well; however, there are matters that need to be discussed. For example, what will we do with Ruth's corpse? We can't leave it out on display much longer; the house will smell of her rot."

"We'll have to bury her," I stated flatly.

"Fair enough. Now, do you think the reason Joseph was so upset with us was because of the situation with her sister?"

"Certainly," I affirmed. "Anything else?"

Yuuto grinned, shifting his weight between his feet. "I'm through with the flirting and secret kisses. I know what you see in Helen. She is remarkable, and I'd hate to do anything behind her back. Whatever it is between us, we'll keep it on hold, yes? For her sake?"

I examined his stance before crossing my arms, forcing a smile. *"A captivating settlement you aren't interested in. Will you agree anyway, for her sake?"* She wondered. I glared at Her as She skimmed Her fingers behind Yuuto's shoulders, gliding Her lips against his hair and giggling maniacally once She sensed my anger. "Agreed," I spat, relief washing over me as She vanished. Yuuto looked behind him, crossing his arms before turning back to me.

"Now, we need to find Joseph. She wouldn't go to her home or the church; it's much too easy."

"How do we know she wouldn't go to either place anyway?"

"It's not worth the risk, she's a killer on the run, and unlike most murderers, she doesn't know what will happen to her if she is caught. She can't afford to hide somewhere predictable."

"Would she go to her sister?" Yuuto offered.

I pondered the thought. "Possibly. She may seek comfort from her sister, or tell her what's happened, so it's likely she's gone there. However, we don't know where her sister lives."

"But we do." Yuuto smiled.

"How?"

"The address, remember? There was an address on one of Ruth's notes. It may be Joseph's brother-in-law!" Yuuto bounced with excitement, proud of his observation.

"Then we need to find it, and prepare Ruth so we may bury her."

I swung my feet at a steady rhythm while I waited for my milkshake, humming a soft tune to myself as I scanned the symphony laid out before me. "Do you play?" the man behind the counter asked me. I looked up and nodded.

"The piano, yes. I learned so I could play while my sister sang," I told him.

The man raised an eyebrow. "A sister? Are you related to Ivory by any chance?"

I proudly sat up while my head bounced in approval. "Have you heard her sing?"

"She performed on that stage there before she got big," the man said. I turned around and stared at the wooden stage at

the back of the parlor. *"The voice of an angel, that one."* He finished, leaving the counter as he attended to another customer. I stared at the stage and pictured my older sister wearing a long red gown, filling the room with her voice.

The man returned and handed me my milkshake, which I took thankfully. As I was about to take my first sip, A girl stumbled into the parlor, her arm caked with dried blood and her left eye swollen. Dirty tear stains covered her cheeks as she sniffled and sat next to me, patting down her messy hair. Her right shoe was missing and the hem of her dress was ripped, as were her gloves.

Her eyes were glossy as she sighed deeply and ordered a vanilla milkshake, the same as mine. Without hesitation, I pushed mine in front of her. She flinched at the action, then stared at me skeptically. *"What do you want?"* she asked huskily, as though someone had thrown rocks at her voice.

"Have mine. It's a busy day today, so it will take him a while, and you don't seem like you want to stay here for much longer, so take mine." The girl knitted her brows, still unsure of my offer. *"I didn't do anything to it. He gave it to me just as you were walking in. Here, to show I mean no harm, you can take my jacket, so you can cover up."*

"I don't want your jacket," she spat. "I don't care what these people think of me. If I'm disturbing them they can leave."

I studied her expression and decided I approved her way of thinking. "I don't see why you'd be disturbing them, you're doing nothing wrong."

The girl fought to hold back a smile. "You're right, I'm merely existing."

"You only want a milkshake, what's wrong with that?"

She took the shake into her hands and took a long drink, sighing afterward. "Nothing at all," she stated matter-of-factly.

"May I ask why you're in such physical disarray?" I questioned.

The girl wiped her mouth with the back of her hand while she turned to face me. "A group of boys fought me. This time I promise I didn't do anything to provoke it. They simply hate me at this point, and so we got into a brawl."

"How did they end up?" I asked.

She laughed at my question, shaking her head. "Worse. Why are you here?"

"I wanted a milkshake."

"That's not what I mean. I'm asking why you are here, with me."

I thought for a moment. "Because you're a pretty girl who was unjustly attacked and deserves a milkshake and some friendly company."

The girl furrowed her eyebrows as she took another long sip of the milkshake I gave her. "You think I'm pretty?"

My heart broke at the question. Had no one told her she was pretty before? How could she be so painfully unaware? "I know you are. You're absolutely stunning, bloodied and all. My name is Walter, by the way."

The girl relaxed her shoulders, grinning as she placed her chin on her right hand. "Hello, Walter, my name's Ruth."

I stared at the patch of dirt that covered Ruth's body, shivering. It hadn't settled until that moment that Ruth was, in fact, extremely dead. Helen intertwined her hand with mine, gently squeezing it as she pressed her lips to my arm.

"Walter, would you like to say anything?" Yuuto whispered.

I hesitantly nodded before pulling away and facing the three people in front of me. "When I first met Ruth, she walked into an ice cream parlor with a swollen eye and a bleeding arm. I never thought that the last time I saw her would be in a similar way," I choked, trying to control my breathing. I turned to face the dirt, pretending Ruth could hear me. "I never wanted you to be perfect, Ruth. I never thought you were. I was amazed that someone with a life like yours managed to turn it around and become an inspiration for others, a beacon of hope, but you didn't have to be for me to love you," I choked, suddenly unable to hold back my tears. I heard Ethel sniffle behind me, and I felt my entire body begin to shake. "You didn't have to be everyone's favorite or the happiest person I knew. You just had to be yourself, whoever that was. I'm terribly sorry you thought you had to please me. I'm sorry you thought that was your purpose. Wherever you may be now, I hope that it is better than the life you lived here. I hope that it's yours."

My chest grew tight as I stepped away, grabbing Helen's hand as I silently cried. Memories of Ruth stumbling into my apartment with bruises washed through my mind, the gentle smile she offered as she asked for a milkshake as if that would make life better. I pictured her sitting on my couch as she watched me make dinner and told me about how once again she didn't do anything to the idiotic boys that attacked her every now and then, and that it caught her by surprise. A part of me thought she might have been lying, that the three boys might have just been one; but I feared asking would drive her away, so instead, I listened intently and spoke at the proper times. Asking questions such as, "What do the boys look like?" and "Why do they always hurt you?" resulted in her becoming mute, as though answering would be the death of her. I wished I had never told her what her smile meant to me, I wish I had never told her she inspired me. She wouldn't have died if she didn't have to lie, would she? Was this my fault?

"Walter, we're going back in. We'll give you a moment to say goodbye alone."

I was far from ready to say goodbye. I felt as though there was more I could have done to help her, more than milkshakes and kind words. I wondered if even now, there's something I could do, anything to make up for the bruises and the troubles she endured by herself.

"*Say something nice.*" She offered. And She was right. "You're not the happiest person I know, Ruth, nor the brightest. But if it weren't for you I wouldn't have met them." I knelt down and placed my palm against the soil, closing my eyes. I hoped she would be able to listen. "I'll say something nice to you now, Ruth. The only person who deserved your kindness more than I did was you."

And with that, I knew I could leave.

Chapter Eleven:

The Case Resumes

"Charles is outside. Will we be taking everyone?" Helen asked.

"I'm returning to my home. I have left my information with Walter. Once again, I apologize about the vase," Ethel stuttered between her words, chewing her bottom lip. I smiled and took her hand, gently kissing it.

"I'm terribly sorry for the misunderstanding, I was far too rash coming to my conclusion. It was an amateur thing to do," I stated.

Yuuto hugged Ethel as he stepped into the car, followed by me and finally Helen.

"Where to, sir?" Charles asked from the front. I looked down at the note in my hand and read aloud the address.

"Right away, sir."

Yuuto looked to me wide-eyed, waiting for an explanation.

"Charles has learned his way around the town; he's quite the adventurer. He also has a magnificent memory and incredible navigation skills," I bragged.

"Thank you, sir, but it is only my duty," Charles insisted, chuckling to himself.

"Don't put yourself down, Charles. You're wonderful," Helen complimented. She reached for my hand and kissed my cheek before returning her gaze to the outdoors.

Once we had reached the house, we stepped out of the car and examined the surroundings. The house was made entirely out of wood just as all of the other houses around the area. However, this house seemed older. The house looked out onto the lake and was surrounded by pine trees and other plants, making it seem significantly smaller than it really was. "Look at this house. Really, what was Ruth thinking, building a marble house in the middle of the woods? Everyone else lives in wooden cottages," Yuuto mumbled.

"You must admit, it's a very 'Ruth' thing to do." I shrugged. I told Charles to wait while we made our way to the front entrance. We knocked on the door and waited for someone to arrive.

"Hello?" a female voice questioned as the door slowly opened.

"Good day to you, madame. Are you by any chance related to Father Joseph?" I asked, smiling innocently. Yuuto and Helen stepped aside, not wanting to intimidate the woman.

"He's my brother, why do you ask?" she said, opening the door a tad wider.

"Splendid! Your brother was reported missing after attending a party. We were wondering if we could speak to you? We were told the two of you are very close, so we assumed you might have some information that could help us," I said in a chipper manner.

The woman swung the door open as her right hand reached for her lips. "Are you the police?" she whispered.

"Yes, this is Yuuto and Helen, my assistants in the case. May we come in?"

The woman placed her hand on the top of her chest, nodding quickly as she moved to the side, allowing us to enter. Yuuto and Helen thanked her softly as they followed my lead. The woman stood next to me as she led us to what seemed to be the living room, gesturing for us to sit on a loveseat placed in front of a coffee table.

"How may I help you?" she asked, dragging a dining chair into the room and sitting down. She wore a maroon skirt, with a white shirt tucked into it. Her curled, black hair reached just above her chin, and dark circles formed under her eyelids.

"When was the last time you saw your brother?" I asked kindly, not wanting her to grow suspicious of me.

"Possibly a week ago, he came to visit my husband and me."

"What for?"

"Oh, just to catch up. He'll stop by monthly to chat with us."

"Where is your husband now? Is he close to Joseph?"

The woman hesitated before shaking her head. "No, Joseph and my husband rarely talk, but they get along fine. He's currently at work."

"What does your husband do for a living?"

"He runs the bar in town." She smiled. "I'm sure you've seen him. It's one of the most popular places there."

"I haven't had the chance to go, but I'll make sure to visit. Now, were you aware of your brother's disappearance?"

Her smile dropped and she shook her head. "No, it's the first I've heard of this," she said.

"You don't seem very concerned," I accused.

The woman folded her hands over her skirt, though she didn't respond. I took this as a sign to proceed.

"I'll ask again: how is the relationship between Joseph and your husband?"

"They get along fine."

"How about your husband and Ruth?" Yuuto interrupted. Both Joseph's sister and I looked to him, shocked at the question.

"Pardon me, but how is that any of your business?" she exclaimed.

I turned to the woman and extended my hand, placing my other arm around Yuuto. "Yuuto, that was unnecessary," I hissed at him before turning to Joseph's sister. "I apologize profusely on his behalf."

"What is this all really about?" The woman shivered.

I took a deep breath. "A day ago, your sister, Joseph, attended Ruth's party. Moments after the party began, Ruth was found dead." At this, the woman gasped, standing from her seat while choking back a sob. "We have concluded that the killer is your sister, Joseph."

Joseph's sister turned away from us, crying into her hands before stuttering, "Joseph came by some hours ago. She said she was leaving because she was in danger of being caught. She said someone found out she was transgender and she had to flee. I can't believe she would . . ." I walked over to the woman and embraced her, caressing her back as I let her cry onto my shoulder.

"Joseph sent a letter to Ruth, warning her that she was going to die. Ruth then set up a party and invited the people she thought would most likely kill her, but what I found interesting is that you weren't invited, your sister was. She was also the most eager to leave the house. We believe she may also have killed Edward Lee Alton, Ruth's butler," I said slowly and softly, not wanting to overwhelm the lady. "If I don't find her, Joseph will be in grave danger. I do not wish to send her to prison or to turn her in. I was told to take care of her and protect her but still punish her accordingly. If you love your sister and wish for her safety, I will need you to help me figure out where she may be now."

Joseph's sister eventually pulled away and nodded, facing the ground the entire time. "I know Ruth and my husband were in love, and there was nothing I could do about it. Whenever I left the house to tend the bar in town, my husband and Ruth would be here, even after I found them together. They briefly stopped their meetings on my behalf, but recently began seeing each other again. No matter what I did, my husband continued to visit her, no longer at our house but at hers. I called Joseph one night and told her everything, unsure of what to do. She said she would take care of it, and last week it ended. My husband stopped seeing her, and a few days after Ruth came to apologize and wished me happiness. I asked her why she decided to end things, and she said she'd soon have to pay for her sins." The woman paused. "Did Ruth know Joseph was going to kill her?"

"She knew she would be killed, but didn't know by who. Yuuto, did she do anything like this before she died?"

Yuuto shook his head. "She apologized for being judgmental about Eddie and me, but that was long ago."

I nodded. "She said she would have to pay for her sins, so she apologized to those she still owed one to; she apologized to Ethel and Liza last week. I'm curious as to why she apologized to Joseph's sister but not Joseph herself."

"Joseph didn't kill Ruth for her own benefit. She did it out of revenge for her sister; there was no reason Ruth had to apologize to Joseph," Helen stated.

"What's your name?" Yuuto asked.

"Reina. And my husband is Abe," Joseph's sister answered.

"Wonderful names. Now how is Abe and Joseph's relationship?"

Reina fumbled with her dress. "Terrible. Ever since Joseph found out about the affair, she's been furious; her temper flared when she last came and found out they had resumed their meetings."

"How did that make you feel?" Yuuto urged.

"To be completely honest, I'm not certain. I'm devastated, but I can't bring myself to care anymore. I know Abe holds no love for me any longer, and I hold none for him. But I can't leave him, not until I know I'll survive."

"Goodness, no one has a working marriage," Yuuto mumbled, earning a nudge from both Helen and me. "Sorry, that was rude. So you don't care about Abe anymore?"

"I care about him, we're somewhat friends, but I no longer see him as a husband."

"Does Joseph know this?" Yuuto inquired.

Reina paused. "No. Last I spoke to Joseph I . . ." Reina's voice faded as her expression changed drastically, her bottom lip quivering as her shoulders grew tight.

"What happened?" I asked.

"I said I wished they were dead."

Shivers ran through my body at her confession. "I—do you think your husband may be in danger?" I stuttered.

Reina stared at me, her shoulders visibly shaking. "I don't know."

I turned to face Yuuto and Helen. "We need to get to Abe, *now*."

I stormed into the bar, looking for a priest.

"Is Abe here?" Helen asked from behind me. A man who loomed over a table looked over and waved.

"That would be me. Is there something wrong?" he asked, approaching us.

"Look at that, he's still alive." Yuuto sighed. Helen rolled her eyes and hit the back of his head.

"Hello, Abe, I'm Detective Walter N. Grover, and these are my assistants. We believe you may be in danger. Have you come in contact with a man named Father Joseph sometime in the past twenty-four hours?"

Abe blinked rapidly before gesturing for us to follow him, leading us to the kitchen.

"Is Joseph alright?" Abe whispered as he closed the door behind us.

"I don't think it's Joseph's safety you should be worrying about, Abe," Yuuto uttered, standing by my side. "Have you seen Joseph?"

Abe flinched before nodding. "Joseph came in maybe one or two hours ago, asked for a drink."

Yuuto burst out laughing to which Helen scowled, immediately pulling him behind her.

I sighed, crossing my arms. "Did Joseph say anything to you?"

"No, just got their drink and left, said it was going to be a busy day."

Helen mumbled something under her breath as I sighed. "I'm terribly sorry, Abe, but Ruth has been murdered. Joseph killed her yesterday."

Abe stepped back, rubbing his hand against his chest as his eyes grew distant. He then began to flex his fingers, baring his teeth as he spoke. "If she was killed yesterday, why was I just informed?"

"Only today did we learn who killed Ruth. It is a subject that is meant to remain undercover. I have here—"

"A subject meant to remain *undercover*? I should have been one of the first people to find out! I should have been told the second she died!" Abe interrupted, his face reddening as his voice grew louder.

"I have here a letter from Ruth that is meant for you. You were not informed because we didn't know she had a relationship with you, not until we spoke to Joseph," I replied calmly.

Abe took the letter but didn't open it. "Joseph did this?" he growled.

I ignored his question. "Per Ruth's request, we wish to find Joseph and place her under my custody. Ruth specifically asked me to protect her killer, so no harm can go Joseph's way. That is why I need to find Joseph before someone else does," I spoke rapidly, hoping anything I said would reassure the broken man.

Abe took a deep breath before shutting his eyes. "I don't know where Joseph is. Have you spoken to her sister, Reina?"

"We have."

"I don't know where she's gone, or where she'd be. If I did, I'd tell you in a heartbeat," he assured us, squeezing the letter in his hand.

"Walter, we have to leave. We need to keep searching," Helen insisted. She turned to Abe and offered a pitiful smile. "I'm terribly sorry for your loss," she said sincerely, then left the kitchen with Yuuto. I stayed behind.

"Ruth was my best friend. In all the years I've known her, I've never come across anyone as wonderful as her. She deserved so much better, and I promise you, I will serve her justice," I said softly.

Before I could turn to leave, Abe grabbed my shoulders and pulled me into a hug. "She meant the world to me. It's a terrible thing, being in love with someone when you're married to someone else, but I couldn't prevent it. If I had known being with Ruth would be her demise, I would have never seen her again. Joseph killed her because of me, because I insisted on meeting her again and again, and the more I did, the more it broke Reina's heart, but I couldn't help myself. I was an idiot."

I held Abe closer, patting his back as he trembled. "This wasn't your fault, don't blame yourself. What you both did was wrong, but it was not worth her life." I thought about Yuuto. I thought about it being him who was killed instead of Ruth, and my heart dropped. "Joseph will pay accordingly for her crime, I promise you. But from here on out you and Reina must pretend Ruth never existed, in order to keep everyone she ever met safe. This is your chance at a new life. You must move forward; it's what Ruth would have wanted for you."

Abe stared at me, unsure of what to say. I moved away, leaving him in the kitchen as I left to meet with Helen and Yuuto outside.

We returned to Reina's house, deciding she would know where Joseph would most likely run. Once Yuuto got out of the car, I began to slide out until Helen grabbed my arm. "I want to speak with you. Ask Yuuto to get a list of the locations by himself," she ordered silently. I examined her face before nodding, passing the instruction to Yuuto, who nodded and left.

"Is something wrong?" I asked her. Helen ignored my question and asked Charles to step out of the car. He obliged.

Helen slumped back on the seat, sighing loudly before facing me. "How much did you truly care about Ruth?"

The question caught me off guard, causing me to jump back slightly. "I cared for her deeply."

"She's dead. You do understand that, don't you? She isn't coming back."

"I'm aware."

"Are you? How have you managed to solve this case in two days and responsibly seek justice without letting your emotions interfere?" Helen sighed once more, leaning out to grab my hand. "Walter, you're an emotional man. You sympathize with those around you and have a heart of gold. Yet, the person you claim to love most in all this world is dead, and you've been managing just fine. How?"

I pulled my hand away and stared at the window beside her, wishing I could jump out as I have many times before. I knew she was right, and there was no possible way I was going to leave the car without answering her question. "I think . . . I think because it feels as though someone else has died. As if the person we buried wasn't Ruth at all."

Helen knit her brows, unsatisfied with my answer. "Did she do something to you, something that upset you but you repressed? Look at Yuuto and the others. They all had some sort of negative experience with Ruth, one so horrid that it lessened the pain of her death."

"She was always good to me."

"I don't think she was," Helen snapped. "And I know you know exactly what it is she did. You simply wish not to acknowledge it. You don't have to tell me now nor ever, but do not forget that she is dead and can never make up for what she did to you, so it's better to leave it behind and move on," Helen advised, patting my leg as she looked out the window. I studied the back of her head as if her hair could explain her sudden behavior.

"You've never been like this," I blurted.

"Like what?"

"I don't know, outspoken? Unafraid of sharing your opinion? Something is different about you."

Helen smirked. "You're correct. I know you didn't want me to come to the party. I see that now. And I don't think it has to do with pride. I think you thought I was average, just another lady waiting to please a husband, but I'm not. I simply wanted to make *you* happy, and it appears the only way to do so is to be authentic." She looked to me, her eyes glistening. "I know you don't love me, but I'd like you to. And to gain your love, one must unapologetically be themselves."

I gently grabbed her arm, grinning as I pulled her into a hug, kissing the top of her head until I decided to speak. "Do not ever change a single thing about yourself for others, do you understand? You don't need to gain my love. My love is not worth your identity. Change for your own good. Be yourself for none other than you." Helen giggled as she held my arm, digging her face deeper into me as I placed my chin on her head and smiled. Just then, Yuuto knocked on the door.

"I'm sorry to disturb this moment, but I have a list here that you might be interested in reading. I suggest we head to San Jose," Yuuto spoke, but avoided my gaze by looking down at the list in front of him.

"San Jose? Why so far?" Helen spat, pulling away from me and staring at Yuuto in surprise.

"Calm down, darling. We don't have to *get* there, we just have to *go* there; we'll find Joseph along the way. Reina said she has a friend in San Jose, and it's highly probable Joseph will stay there for some time until you return to London."

I frowned. "And if she isn't going to San Jose?"

"Reina said that it's incredibly likely she will. She also gave me a list of motels and places to stay if we decide to go on the trip."

I thought for a moment before shaking my head. "If Reina has given us enough information, we may be able to find Joseph, but it's a long trip and Joseph has the lead. It may be unlikely we meet her," I decided.

"We could have Reina help us somehow," Helen suggested.

"That may work. Would Reina cooperate?" Yuuto agreed.

I thought about Reina and Abe. *"Reina still loves her sister, but we must convince her that Joseph is in far more danger by herself. She's a criminal on the run, not only that but a transgender priest. If Reina values her sister's life, we can convince her to help us this way,"* She said from the front seat, turning to face me. I stared at Her and thought about Her point. *"What do you say, Detective?"* I grinned and looked to Yuuto and Helen before allowing my gaze to fall back on Her. She smiled with pride, turning to sit properly. "I may have a plan," I announced.

Chapter Twelve:

Familiar Reformation

Reina set out a map in front of Charles, describing the route we should take on our way to San Jose as I waited in her living room. I raised the teacup before me to my lips, sipping quietly while I stared out the window. A knock on the front door urged me to stand, and I rubbed my eyes while I shuffled to the entrance.

"Is this small enough?" Yuuto asked, holding up his bag. I nodded.

"Helen will be back soon with Abe. She'll be taking longer since she's checking us out of our room," I told him, heading toward the car.

Yuuto smiled softly. "I forget you aren't from around these parts, even though your accent makes it obvious."

I took the bag from his hands and threw it into the trunk of the car, sighing as we headed inside. Charles nodded at the two of us as we made our way into the living room. "When will we leave?" Yuuto asked.

"The moment Charles and Reina are done with the planning. Of course, if they're finished before Helen returns, we'll leave when she's here. The sooner we leave, the greater the chance of finding Joseph will be," I told him, taking another drink from my tea.

"As soon as possible then. Did you sleep, by any chance?"

I nodded. "A short nap, so that I may have more energy when we leave. I'll be driving."

Yuuto raised his eyebrow, sitting on the dining room chair Reina had dragged in earlier in the afternoon. "You're driving?"

"It's almost night. I don't want Charles to deprive himself of sleep for something that does not involve him in the slightest. He may be my chauffeur, but chasing after murderers was certainly not in the job description," I stated.

"Pardon me, sir, I do not mean to eavesdrop, but I must inform you that though road trips to San Jose and criminals are not part of the job, I do not mind at all. I will be the one to take you," Charles said from the door, smiling proudly.

"Charles, thank you so much for the offer, However—"

"He means to say thank you, Charles. We're immensely grateful for your help." Yuuto smiled. He reached for my hand and grabbed it, rolling his eyes jokingly to Charles, who laughed in response.

"Madam Reina has given me a map and directions to get to San Jose. She believes Madam Joseph is currently at a cottage court and will eventually call Madam Reina in order to inform her of her whereabouts. She suggests we leave as soon as the lady of the house returns." Charles bowed his head as he left the room. Yuuto slowly turned to face me.

"Lady of the house?"

I grinned. "Charles is old fashioned, one of my favorite things about him. He's a very respectable man."

Yuuto bit his lip. "I'll say," he said, resulting in laughter.

"An entire year together. Can you believe it?" Ruth giggled, her arm wrapped around mine.

I smiled and shook my head, examining the houses we walked past. "It feels much shorter. What would you like to do in order to honor such a pleasant day?"

Ruth pondered for a second before her eyes lit up with a response. "We should head to your place and have a few drinks. What better way to celebrate?" I nodded in agreement as we headed to my house, my grip on Ruth tightening slightly as our pace quickened.

When we arrived at my house, Ruth quickly kicked off her shoes and raced for a cupboard, pulling out two glasses while I looked for the wine. Once we were ready, we sat on a loveseat in the living room and began to drink, laughing as we spoke of old memories and told stories we had long forgotten. As the night grew older, our consciousness faded, until I was lying on the floor, my left arm draped on the sofa, while Ruth slouched on the loveseat.

"Walter?" she slurred.

"Hm?" I answered, looking up. She shifted in her seat, the leg she had lazily placed at the arm of the chair pulling away as she sat up.

"Walter," she hummed again, giggling after.

I smiled as she rubbed at her eyes, her grin growing larger as she let her head fall back. "Yes, Ruth?"

She looked over to me, her eyes glazed. "I love you."

I grinned and tapped her hand, sitting up myself. "I know, I love you too."

Ruth shook her head. "No, you silly boy," she chuckled, taking both of my hands. My brows furrowed but my smile remained. "I'm in love with you, don't you see? But you can't know, because then you'll want to wed, and I can't." She briefly stopped her confession as she hiccuped. "Ever since we first spoke you've been so sweet, no one's been sweet before, and I can't lose you, I can't." She hiccuped again. "Wait and see, Walter. When I get the money I'm going to buy a pretty house near the mountains and leave him and everyone behind, and I'll be sweet just like you. Don't let me forget it, please. I'm going to be the nicest person in the world, just like you. Okay?"

I stared at Ruth, frowning as I attempted to understand what she was saying between her slurs. "You'll be like what?" I asked, my drunken mind unable to process her words.

"Like you. I'll be nice just like you, and you'll be proud. It'll all be for you."

"Okay, I won't forget," I mumbled, falling asleep.

I forgot.

Abe took the bag from Helen while I sat in the front next to Charles, leaving Helen and Yuuto by themselves in the back seat. Reina gave us last-minute advice and hugged me tightly, asking me to take good care of her sister. Abe walked by after her, telling me to make sure Joseph paid for her crimes. As we pulled away from the driveway, Abe and Reina waved from their doorstep, Abe's arm wrapped around Reina's shoulders. I looked to him and smiled, wishing he could see my face.

"When will the first break be?" Yuuto asked. Helen laughed while I rolled my eyes.

"Yuuto, we're not even a minute into this trip. What do you need?"

"I'm only asking because Charles will need to sleep at some point, so I'm willing to drive for the rest of the way to our first stop when he decides to rest."

I shook my head. "No need, I've already offered to drive for Charles when needed."

"I forgot you know how to drive," Helen said with surprise.

I chuckled. "Of course I can. What do you think I did before Charles?"

Yuuto leaned back, placing his arms behind his head. "How did Charles come into the picture? Having a chauffeur is for those with money."

Charles smiled nervously and looked to me, making sure his reaction was not offensive. "Charles used to work for Helen's family, but he offered to work for us once Helen and I married. Can you imagine what it was like explaining to the other officers why a chauffeur brought me to work in the morning?" We all laughed, imagining the conversation.

"Helen, if I may ask, is your family wealthy?"

"Somewhat, it's something I do not like to talk about. We're not famous or anything, but we have a popular business," was all Helen admitted to.

I looked behind and saw Helen resting her head against the window, her face expressionless. Yuuto smiled lazily as he began to close his eyes, signaling he was going to sleep. I decided that would be a good idea and followed suit.

It was hard to tell what time it was once I woke up, but Charles's eyes were fluttering as he looked out onto the road and Yuuto quietly snored from the back seat. Helen's head bobbed against the window, which I imagined would be painful if she were conscious. "Charles, pull over. I'll drive."

"Are you sure, sir?" he asked, his voice groggy.

"If you keep driving you'll fall asleep and crash. It's alright, Charles, I'll take it from here," I insisted. Charles pulled over and showed me where we were just before we switched seats. After we switched places, Charles lifted his feet to the seat and curled up into a ball, immediately falling asleep. I looked out and noticed the emptiness of the roads, watching the occasional tree or bush rush past as I drove. The repetitive view mesmerized me as I struggled not to fall asleep. It was a sudden intake of air and muffled groans from the back seat that caused me to awaken.

"How long have you been driving?" Helen asked hoarsely.

"Charles and I switched some time ago. When did you wake up?" I asked, not taking my eyes off the road.

"Just now. My head was beginning to hurt. How close are we?"

I looked at the map placed on the dashboard. "We should arrive by dawn, earlier if we're lucky. You can go back to sleep."

Helen stretched. "No, I'll keep you company. Besides, I'd like to talk to you."

"Again? Last time we did that it wasn't a very pleasant conversation."

"But a necessary one. How are you feeling?"

I shrugged. "Tired."

"Well, you haven't properly slept in two days. Practically three now," Helen mumbled.

I rolled my eyes, growing irritated. "I'm on a case. I'm always tired when I'm on a case. This is no exception."

"Ah, so you are dissociating, treating this entire situation as just another case, so you'll stay on track? Very clever," she said.

"Please stop. It's too early for this. I'll grieve when there's time."

"You aren't a machine, Walter. You don't have to be strong at all times and cry silently to yourself when no one is looking. That's not who you are. You can talk about your feelings, you can share them. The person who handed you this burden is dead. You don't have to keep it. We don't have to find Joseph."

I continued to look at the road, thinking about her words. A part of me knew she was right. I could easily return to Lake Tahoe, make plans to return to England, pretend nothing happened. I could continue my life with Helen or sort a new one with Yuuto. I didn't have to be driving to San Jose in the dark with my chauffeur, my wife, and Yuuto. "But I want to," I answered, to both Helen and myself. "I want to end this. I don't want to live the rest of my life thinking I could have done better for Ruth, I don't want . . ." I gulped and blinked away my tears. "I don't want to fail her, or worse, myself."

"Do you miss her?"

I sat silently. "I do. So much." My voice broke as I gripped the steering wheel. "Too much."

"Then why haven't you cried?"

"We all cope differently," Yuuto voiced groggily. His sudden involvement in the conversation surprised me, provoking me to wonder when the soft snores had come to an end. "When my family kicked me out, I didn't cry, though it was a terrible loss. Granted they did not die, but it felt as though they did. I haven't cried, not even now. But I screamed, I grew angry, I dealt with drugs and got into trouble as much as I could because I couldn't believe it; the people who had been there for me my entire life, gone in the blink of an eye. Walter here overworks himself, searches for answers in order to satisfy his endless questions. He is searching for a conclusion to his nightmare, and I for one am more than willing to assist."

"Have you moved on?" I asked. A tear trickled down my cheek.

"I have now, but it took years."

"How?" Helen asked.

I felt Yuuto's eyes land on the back of my head, and my face flushed.

"Simple, I found a better family," he answered assuringly.

After a moment of quiet, we resumed talking, speaking softly in order not to wake Charles from his sleep. It wasn't until we noticed the sunrise from the east that we were nearing our first destination. "What will we do once we arrive?" Helen asked me.

"We can't do much other than rest; we'll leave in the afternoon. Reina promised to call me once we arrive at the cottage courts." We all looked at the road and searched for the cottage courts Reina had mentioned, until we finally came across what looked like a village.

Small, identical houses lined up close to each other, surrounded by patches of well-watered grass. The houses were all red with two windows on the side; it appeared all of the houses had a single room and were separated by an empty space meant for a car.

"Tourist court, or cottage court as Reina called them. I have never seen one myself," Yuuto said in awe. We pulled over to a large house not far from the court and assumed the owner lived there.

"What will we do with Charles?" Helen asked.

"Let him sleep. I'll go out and see if anyone's home," I answered, getting out of the car. I stretched my legs before walking up the driveway and knocking on the front door.

"Yes?" a woman responded. She wore a knee-length plaid skirt with a white long-sleeved shirt tucked inside of it. Her curled, blonde hair cascaded onto her shoulders, and her smile reached her ears. The sudden wave of warmth and comfort radiating from the woman took me by surprise.

"Do you own the courts?" I stuttered.

The woman smiled at my flustered expression.

"My husband does, yes. Is it just you?"

"No, I—we need two cottages I suppose. My wife and I will share one, my two friends will share another one. Are there any available?" I asked nervously.

The woman nodded, looking to the courts. "Any cabin without a car is open. The key is under the mat. Do make sure to return it once you leave. Breakfast is served at eight thirty, lunch is at twelve, and dinner is at seven." As she began to close the door, I quickly moved my arm and held the door open.

"I'm sorry, one more question. Is there a phone in the cabins? Or one I may use?"

The woman nodded. "There's one inside. Do you need it now?"

I looked to the car and noticed Yuuto and Helen whispering to each other while Charles slept, his feet on the dashboard and his chin tucked into his chest. "No, it's still too early, but I'd like to use it later in the day if that's alright." The woman nodded and waited for any further questions before bidding me farewell and shutting the door. It wasn't until that very moment I realized just how early it was, and shuffled to the car in embarrassment.

"Who was that?" Yuuto asked once I got into the car.

"The wife of the owner. She said there are keys underneath the mats, forgot to ask about the price though. We'll get two cabins. Yuuto and Charles can share. Is that alright?"

Yuuto looked to Charles and smiled, nodding. I instantly looked away and took a deep breath, feeling my skin begin to burn. "Wonderful," I said acidly, surprised at my anger. Yuuto snorted as if to tell me he found joy in my jealousy.

After parking between two empty cabins, Charles awoke and sleepily walked into his cottage, Yuuto following behind with both of their bags. I pulled out the luggage and walked past Helen, who was holding the door to our room open.

The cottage had one room and a bathroom that held the smallest shower I had ever seen. The floors were made of wood and the bed was relatively small, almost not big enough for two people. I wondered if it was similar for Yuuto and Charles.

I chewed the inside of my cheeks at the thought.

"Is something wrong?" Helen asked as she took out a nightgown from the bag.

I looked up and forced a smile, shaking my head. "No, it's all fine. Just thinking."

"What about?" she asked, beginning to change.

I walked past her and looked into the bag, quickly thinking of some sort of excuse. "The case, I'm hoping we'll be able to find Joseph soon enough," I lied. Though it was partially true, I worried we wouldn't be able to find Joseph in time.

Helen scoffed, but not in an annoyed manner. "You have to stop worrying, Walter. Everything will be fine."

"I hope so," I muttered, pulling out pajamas. Helen placed her hands on top of mine, stopping me from moving. She lifted my chin and gently kissed my lips, stroking the back of my neck as she grinned.

"I *know* so," she assured me, kissing me once more before walking to the bed, smiling. I changed rapidly and joined her.

I looked at the glass of wine before me, which I had only taken two sips of. "To you, Walter, and your future," Ruth said, interrupting my meaningless thoughts. I looked up and smiled, lifting my glass. "I wish you all the luck in the world."

We intertwined our arms and took a drink, before returning to our silence. We both knew to speak would erupt into an unpleasant conversation; therefore we chose to stay quiet. However, Ruth did not seem to enjoy our silent agreement.

"How's Helen?" Ruth asked. I stopped chewing my food.

"Well. Preparing for the wedding," I stated simply.

Ruth nodded, the question she longed to ask stuck in her throat. "I'm glad."

"You are invited," I reminded her. "You can come."

Ruth shook her head. "I can't, Walter."

"Why not?"

Ruth looked up to me with saddened eyes. "I just can't." I decided pressing questions would result in an uncomfortable and unnecessary conversation; therefore I allowed the silence to resume.

"How's Ruby?" she blurted. The silence was nice while it lasted.

I looked up to her and cocked my head to the side, sighing deeply to show my annoyance. "I don't know. I haven't spoken to her."

"She's not invited?" Ruth shamefully asked.

"I'm getting remarried. To another woman. After five years of marriage with her and . . . why the hell would I invite her?"

Ruth stared at me as the bottom of her lip quivered. She pushed back her shoulders before responding, "Because you're all she has left."

"We don't know that anymore. She could have found someone else."

"How likely is that?"

I glared at her. "I'm not inviting her."

Ruth shrugged. "I don't mean to start a war, Walter. I'm simply stating that she should be able to know that you are in a much better place, that she did right by allowing you to leave."

My chest grew light as I clenched my fists unconsciously. "She didn't allow me to leave, she was furious."

"I talked to her. She told me what happened," Ruth calmly admitted.

"When did you talk to her?" I hissed, almost jumping to my feet.

Ruth sighed as she fumbled with the edge of the table, regretting her confession instantly. "A month or so ago. She's doing well, by the way. She said you two haven't spoken in some time."

"Why did you call her?" I asked.

Ruth forced a laugh, covering her mouth with the back of her hand as she looked out the window. "I didn't call her. And do lower your voice, we are in a restaurant," she whispered nervously.

"She called you?"

Ruth shook her head, looking to me again. "It doesn't matter, Walter, I just . . ." She lowered her hands, most likely clasping them together under the table. "Why did you lie? Why did you say she was upset?"

I looked at my wine glass and felt my chest compress as my legs grew stiff. My breathing quickened, my gaze becoming blurry. I furrowed my eyebrows as my entire body grew numb, holding me hostage to the conversation. Ruth asked something, but her words sounded slurred as they entered my ears, escaping just as quickly as they were muttered. After what seemed like an eternity of attempting to breathe, my muscles relaxed and I was freed from the stiff prison I had unknowingly been placed in. "I have to go. It's getting late," I lied. I threw a few pounds onto the table and gathered my belongings, refusing to look at Ruth directly.

"Walter, I didn't call her. I promise I didn't. I'm only worried."

I looked at the people around us. There were a few couples who were whispering in our directions, probably theorizing what had just happened.

"Walter, please sit down. You're causing a scene."

This is why I asked for quiet. This is why I insisted on silence. Ruth is a walking timebomb, a beautiful chaotic mess ready to explode with drama at any given time, especially with topics that shouldn't be talked about.

"I won't bring Her up again. I'll never say Her name again, I promise." *Ruth practically threw herself at my feet, tugging down at my shirt.*

"I have to go."

"I'll never bring Her up again," *Ruth stated as if her life depended on the promise.* "I won't get involved. Please sit down. Don't leave me—"

"It's okay, Ruth. I have to go. This isn't your fault."

"I'm sorry."

"You shouldn't be."

"I am."

"Thank you for coming. You're still invited to the wedding, by the way. But if I don't see you at the wedding, then I wish you safe travels now."

"Say something nice?" Ruth asked desperately.

I smiled. "You look beautiful tonight."

When I woke up it was about one in the afternoon. I lazily turned and faced Helen, who was sleeping peacefully beside me. I grinned and kissed her forehead before slowly getting out of the bed, stretching before taking a hasty shower and getting dressed. I tiptoed out of the cottage and looked around, wondering what to do. "Shouldn't you call Reina? It's almost two," Yuuto's voice came from beside me. I smiled widely as I turned to face Yuuto, putting my hands into my pockets. He pressed the cigar between his fingers on the ground, putting out the light.

"Were you able to sleep?" I asked, the only words I could conjure up.

"A bit. Charles and I had a very pleasant conversation early this morning before going to sleep."

My arms tensed. I took a deep breath and attempted to convince myself I didn't care. But I knew I did. I cared *so very much*. "What about?" I asked nonchalantly.

Yuuto chuckled, looking straight ahead, not buying my act. "You."

I choked back a gasp, staring at him wide-eyed. "Me? Why?" I stuttered, rubbing my right thumb against my index finger.

"You and Helen, really. Just about your life with her, what you're both like. I've learned quite a few things about you."

"Like what?"

"You've been married to her for a year, you both get along splendidly despite the arguments you both seem to have constantly. She's quiet and obedient until recent events, where she seems to be more sure of herself and speaks out a lot. You, on the other hand, have a cliché habit of bottling up all your emotions, and it's something that irritates Helen and at times Charles." He looked over to me, smiling plainly. "So nothing I didn't already know."

I examined his eyes, bursting into laughter as I turned to face him and hugged him tightly, taking in his warmth and smell. "You're so bothersome."

Yuuto pressed his smile against my neck. "I know. But you love it," he whispered. He pulled away and looked to the owner's home. "You should call Reina."

I gazed at him, resisting the urge to take his hand. "Come with me. I don't want to go alone."

"You mean you just want my company."

"That's a possibility," I answered.

Yuuto rolled his eyes, his grin widening, which seemed almost impossible. I instantly took note that I loved his smile like that, and made it my mission to make sure I could make him grin that way at least twice a day. "You idiot. Let's go."

Chapter Thirteen:

Just One Call

"It's you again! Good afternoon, did you rest well?" the woman asked the moment she opened the door.

I nodded and thanked her, introducing her to Yuuto.

"I assume you need to use the phone now?"

"Yes, please. Also, I'm terribly sorry for disturbing you this morning. It hadn't dawned on me how early it was," I apologized.

"It's alright. We've had guests stop by much earlier than you. Please, come inside."

I thanked the woman and stepped forward, Yuuto following close behind. "I never got around to asking for your name," I remembered.

"Mrs. Mallory. The phone is this way," she cheerfully said, examining Yuuto and me. Yuuto gave me a side glance, to which I frowned.

"What is it?" I whispered, leaning into him.

Yuuto smiled and looked ahead, his expression plain. "I don't think she has a husband."

My eyes went wide. "You can't say things like that, Yuuto. It's improper. Besides, it's not kind to theorize about other's lives," I scolded. "But I'm curious, what do you mean? Her husband died?"

Yuuto snorted. "I think she has a *wife*," he said, looking toward Mrs. Mallory.

I gaped at his statement and looked around. "She can't possibly have a wife. Besides, how did you come to that conclusion?"

Mrs. Mallory opened a pair of doors that seemed to lead to a living room. The walls were lined with shelves overflowing with papers and books. A study desk was placed in the center, piles of documents spread neatly on top. Next to the papers sat a phone. "This is my husband's study, though he won't mind you using the phone, but be quick, he will be needing this office soon."

Before she could leave, Yuuto raised his hand and stepped in front of Mrs. Mallory. "Pardon me, but is there another lady who lives in this house? I thought I saw someone earlier today, but I was uncertain."

Mrs. Mallory's expression brightened, her smile growing. "Yes, my good friend Charity. She helps us maintain the tourist courts."

Yuuto nodded, looking over to me. "A good friend." He walked over and slipped his hand into mine, picking up the phone with his other hand. "Go on, Walter, call Reina. I'd like to speak with Mrs. Mallory if you don't mind." I lifted my gaze from the telephone to Yuuto, nodding as I took the phone from him and released his hand. Yuuto smiled and walked toward Mrs. Mallory, asking to speak with her outside of the room.

I dialed Reina's number and waited.

"Hello?"

"Reina? It's Walter."

"Walter! I was wondering when you'd call. How are you doing?"

"Well, we arrived at the cottage courts this morning, too early to call you. Yuuto is speaking to Mrs. Mallory, most likely about Joseph. Has she called you?"

A pause. "She did, quickly. She wouldn't tell me where she was, but I made her promise to call me as soon as possible. Stay where you are for now and leave my sister to me. I'll call as soon as I can."

I shifted uncomfortably, resting against the table. "I don't have direct access to the phone. Do you have an idea as to when you might be able to call me?"

"No idea, but three o'clock maybe? Joseph called this morning at ten."

"She's been on the road for a while."

"I got this under control, Walter. I'll attempt to stall her as much as possible. I want my sister to be safe."

"Does she know I'm coming?"

"No, but if she asks me if I know anything, I won't lie to her. She's my sister and I love her. I can't lie to her."

"If you do she won't tell you of her whereabouts any longer. If you care for her safety you must trust me."

"What will happen if you don't find her?"

I sighed. "Ruth specifically ordered me to make sure her killer is kept safe, which implies that Joseph is in danger on her own. I don't know what exactly may be waiting for her, but I do not doubt it will be someone seeking revenge in Ruth's honor. As horrid as Ruth's actions with many may have been, she was still caring and compassionate. She would never wish what happened to her to happen to anyone else. She entrusted me to make sure that no matter what happens, her killer, Joseph, will not be harmed on Ruth's behalf. I don't know what will happen if I don't find her, and for her sake and yours, I suggest we don't find out."

Reina remained quiet, taking in everything I had told her. After a few minutes, I heard a soft mutter. "If you find her and she is hurt, you will pay."

"I know."

"I'll call you soon," Reina stated coldly, hanging up. I gently placed the phone back on its stand and left the room in search of Yuuto. I waited outside the door until I heard voices, more specifically, Yuuto's. I followed the sound until I reached the dining room.

"Walter! What did Reina say?" Yuuto asked. His feet were propped on the table, and in front of him sat Mrs. Mallory with her arm wrapped around who I could only assume to be Charity, a woman with short brown hair. Freckles were scattered over her slightly tanned arms, and she wore a short-sleeved blouse and a pleated skirt.

"She'd call back around three. Joseph called this morning to check in, but no information was offered. Reina said she'd find a way to stall her and demanded we stay longer and wait," I informed him. "I say, what are you doing?"

Yuuto signaled to the ladies in front of him. "Annabelle and Charity here were telling me about themselves. Oh, and Joseph I guess."

I pulled up a chair beside Yuuto and looked to the women. "Do you recall Joseph?"

Charity nodded. "We don't get many priests around here, and he's quite a character. He briefly stopped by yesterday; ate some food and took a nap, then left as fast as he came. He seemed to be in a hurry."

"He's a criminal on the run. Of course he's in a hurry," Yuuto muttered.

"Did he talk to you at all?" I asked, ignoring Yuuto's comment.

Annabelle waved me off, shaking her head. "He was deadly silent. Any time I tried to speak to him he'd say he was sorry but he didn't have time to speak. It was very evident that he was running from someone, but then again it wouldn't be the first time we come across a runner."

"When did he arrive and when did he leave?" Yuuto questioned.

"We assume he left a few hours before you arrived, maybe five? Four?" Charity responded.

"Why did you let him stay, even though he was suspicious?" I asked.

Charity sat forward, looking to Yuuto then me. "If anyone knew about Annabelle and me, we would be targeted and killed instantly. We live in the middle of nowhere where we know we'll be safe. We've housed people just like us for years, people trying to run to safety or run away from danger; we're a safe haven for people like the four of us and others who are not acceptable in the eyes of society."

I looked over to Yuuto, whose hands rested above his lap. His gaze suggested he was lost in thought, and I began to wonder about his family. I thought about everything I'd learned about Yuuto, everything he had done in the past two days. I furrowed my brows as I thought about this being I had come to know, thrown out of his house, disowned by the people he cared about the most. I wondered what he was like when he decided to pursue the path that could have nearly killed him, how Ruth saved him and gave him a second chance just as she had many times before for people with stories like Yuuto's, some kinder or worse. I took his hand into mine and suddenly pecked his cheek. He gasped at the feeling and then smiled, lifting his eyes to the women in front of us, both grinning.

"So Joseph was here, nervous and in a hurry. She must know we're following her. I wonder if she knows Reina is helping?" I whispered to Yuuto, facing away from the women.

Yuuto stared at me with wide eyes, still grinning from my impulsive action. "I—no, I don't think Joseph would assume so. Reina said they're both incredibly close. Besides, it's clear she doesn't trust you just yet," Yuuto stuttered, averting his gaze from me in order to hide his smile.

I looked at Annabelle. "Do you mind if we stay for an hour or so? We must wait for another call." Annabelle shook her head. "Wonderful. I'll go to my wife, Yuuto.

Please stay and wait. I'll be back momentarily." Yuuto nodded, glancing at my lips but immediately turning away.

Annabelle and Brian Mallory, her husband, sat in their living room with Helen and Yuuto, quietly discussing things that normal people talked about, such as the weather, and soon-to-be-normal things, such as the upcoming war.

"I hope that the States don't get involved," I heard Brian state.

"It must be terrible to be here while your country is in danger. I pray for your safety," Annabelle followed. Helen didn't respond to either, most likely giving them a small nod instead of a proper "thank you" in order to emphasize how unhelpful both statements were.

"Is Yuuto your lover?" Charity asked me, sitting on the loveseat across from the desk at which I sat, waiting for the phone to ring. It was a quarter past three, and Reina hadn't said a thing. I looked up to her, wondering if this was a discussion that was necessary.

"I don't know," I responded honestly. "We haven't really talked about it. We're friends for now."

"For now?" Charity questioned.

I nodded. "Until I find Joseph. I'd rather not worry about my relationships while I'm in search of a loose murderer."

Charity smirked. "It looks like you have your priorities straight. But you do love Yuuto?"

"I like him very much. However, I met him two days ago, and since then a war has begun, my best friend and her butler were killed, and I realized that I may have to get divorced for the second time in less than ten years, so it isn't necessarily something I'd like to talk or think about at the moment," I snapped, not realizing until after I had spoken how unnecessary my attitude was. "I'm sorry," I promptly apologized.

"You're under stress. I'm sorry about your friend and their butler," she said soothingly.

"Thank you, and I am, though that does not excuse my behavior as of late," I apologized.

Charity seemed as though there was something she wanted to say, but the phone rang seconds before she could speak. I quickly lifted the phone and raised it to my ear, asking who the caller was. It was Reina.

"Joseph is hours ahead of you, but I think you'll be able to catch her if you hurry. I told her to stay where she is because someone is looking for her, and she must wait for my call so that I may tell her where to go. I'll give you three hours before I call her back. Go now."

"Are you sure she'll stay where she is?" I asked.

"Positive."

"We'll leave immediately. Will three hours be enough time?"

"Enough time to catch up, it's the best I can do without making her suspicious. She has stopped at an old friend's house, so she feels safe and she knows she won't be found there. You have to leave."

She spat out Joseph's location, which I quickly noted, hanging up soon after. I walked past Charity and out of the study, running into the living room where everyone sat. "Yuuto, get Charles. We're leaving now. Reina will be stalling Joseph for the next three hours, so we must take this to our advantage and leave instantly." Yuuto stood up quickly as Helen,'s brows rose, both springing to action at my words. I thanked the Mallorys as I followed close behind them.

***

Charles started the car, yawning while I placed Yuuto's bag into the trunk. "Helen, did you pay?" I asked. Annabelle nodded for her.

"She did. Is there anything we can help you with?"

"Wish us luck." Helen smiled, getting into the car. Annabelle whispered something into Charity's ear, then left with Brian hand in hand.

Charity stepped forward, patting my right arm. "What are you going to do when this is over?"

I looked at the car, where Helen and Yuuto were waiting. I pondered her question before answering honestly, "I'll sort things out with those two as soon as I can."

"Can I offer some advice before you go?" she asked.

I nodded.

"Annabelle, Brian, and I are very happy. He's incredibly good friends with Annabelle; they've known each other since they were kids. He was the first person to know that she liked women; she hasn't discussed it with outsiders. At times Brian leaves and has short affairs under a different name, but he is content. You can ask him yourself. We're all happy with our lives," she said. I furrowed my eyebrows, wondering where she was going with this. "Helen isn't blind. She's incredibly smart from what Annabelle told me. She most likely knows there's something between you two, but she's said nothing. She is waiting for you to bring it up. Isn't that telling?" I continued to stare at her, dumbfounded by what she was proposing. I had no clue as to what to say. "Talk to her. When it's all over, which will be soon enough, talk to her. And remember, no one has to get their heart broken."

"Thank you," was all I could say. However, those two words could not even begin to describe what she had done to me, how it was her fault that hope now flourished within me.

"Take care of yourself, Walter. And take care of them. This is your second chance."

My heart dropped at her final words. She stepped forward and hugged me, and though I tried, I could not muster the strength to hug her back. She offered me a last smile before promptly turning and walking away to join her lover and her best friend.

They did seem very happy indeed.

Chapter Fourteen:

I Just Wanted to Sing Opera

The case was almost over.

"You almost got your killer . . . what then?"

The question was far more layered than intended. A war had begun; therefore I had to prepare for the worst. I would also have to find out what to do with Joseph once she was caught. And to top it all off, I had to figure out what would happen with Helen and Yuuto.

"Think, old boy, who do you love?" She asked from behind. I imagined She was squished between the two She was speaking of, though I refused to look. *"Whatever happens with these two doesn't have to be instant. You don't need to fix this the moment Joseph is found. Take your time,"* She offered. "But with the war coming, how much time do we really have?" I responded. Helen hummed in confusion.

"Did you say something, darling?" Helen asked. It felt like it had been ages since she last called me that. I didn't recoil at the name.

"No, just talking to myself," I said. *"Quite literally, too. Walter, you're almost done with this case, but you aren't done yet. Focus on the present. We can worry about the future some other time."*

"How long has it been?" Yuuto asked, his cheek pressed against his fist while his elbow rested against the car window. I turned to look at him better, examining his far-off look, how he stared out onto the road with wonder and awe. I was suddenly worried I had a proper answer to Her second question.

"An hour and a half, roughly. If Joseph remains in place, we will get close enough," Charles replied.

"We'll have to thank Reina once we find her," Helen muttered.

"We can't. I've decided Joseph cannot learn that Reina helped us, not unless Reina tells her herself. Their bond is too strong. It shouldn't be broken, not when Joseph will need her the most," I countered. "Besides, there is no need to thank Reina. She didn't do this for us. She did this for her sister."

"But Joseph wouldn't understand, not now at least," Charles inquired.

I nodded. "Exactly."

"What will you do once you find Joseph?" Helen wondered.

"We'll have two cars, so I'll take Joseph in one, and Charles can take the other. Yuuto and you can decide who you'd like to return with."

Helen snorted. "I'd rather not come home sitting next to someone who has killed two people in the last two days, thank you."

"Home?" I perked up, shifting to face Helen. She stared at me blankly, not realizing what she had said.

"Sorry, back to Tahoe. Yuuto, do you mind if I go with Charles?"

"Not at all," he said.

I faced the front once more and firmly nodded. "Good, now all I need is a proper plan."

Three hours had officially gone by.

Charles drove as fast as he could, hoping to get as close as possible. As we reached Joseph's location, we noticed a car pulling out of a house and a man waving the car away. At that moment we all knew who it was.

"We're so close," Yuuto whispered. I stayed still.

"Wait a moment, slow down. She can't suspect us," I said, my heart racing.

After a few minutes, Charles resumed to normal speed, almost as nervous about the situation as I was.

"We'll follow her to the next stop. Can everyone hang on until then?" The group nodded. "Good. Once we reach the next stop, it'll be easy to grab her. The possibilities of her being armed are high. I doubt she has a gun of any sort, but we must keep the thought in mind. I will be the first to get out of the car and get her."

It felt as though the road grew longer as we followed Joseph, as though our next destination was years away. We kept a reasonable distance from Joseph, not wanting her to grow weary. However, the thought that she knew we were following her grew stronger as we approached the next stop. It wasn't until we began seeing houses go by that we realized we had already reached our destination.

Helen leaned over and gripped my shoulders as Yuuto inhaled sharply. "If we get out now, she'll run. Keep going," he blurted. I spun around to face him, surprised.

"What do you mean?"

"This is a house, not a cottage court or a hotel. If we stop in front of the house or anywhere near it she'll know it's us and leave instantly. Charles, I need you to keep going, now!" Yuuto raised his voice, hitting the back of Charles's seat. Charles jolted and nodded, passing by the house.

"How will we get her now?" I asked Yuuto, extremely agitated at his sudden decision.

Yuuto glared at me, sitting back in place. "She isn't going anywhere. We'll loop around the neighborhood and return. Then you can go in and get her, but we'll have to surround the place. There may be back doors, so I'll stand in the back in case Joseph tries to make a run for it. I suggest Helen is the one to go up to the door and speak to whoever lives there. Joseph has never seen Helen, and the people in the household won't suspect her. Walter, you wait in the car. If Joseph steps out to talk to Helen, I'm sure she's strong enough to apprehend her, and then you can pop out and help her. Or if things go wrong and Joseph tries to make a run for it, you'll be waiting here and can stop her."

"Apprehend her with *what*?" I questioned.

"I've got some rope in my bag," Yuuto muttered. My eyes grew wide, as did Helen's.

Yuuto examined us both, sighing as if we were complete idiots. "Oh, come on, I used to be a drug dealer and I've been mixed with bad crowds for a large portion of my life. Is this really that surprising?"

Charles took a turn, preparing to go back into the street. I thought about Yuuto's plan, how quickly he had thought about it. It wasn't the first time he had planned something like this. "Charles, go with Yuuto, in case he needs assistance," I stated. I waited for Yuuto to argue, but he didn't.

The second we parked in the driveway, Charles and Yuuto got out from the left side of the car and cowered, tiptoeing to the side of the house and practically crawling their way to the back. I waited until they were out of sight to signal Helen, telling her to get out of the car. I slid down the seat, attempting to hide from anyone's view. "Good luck," I whispered once Helen opened the door. She smiled in response.

Helen wore a tight-fitting suit, decorated with a scarf that was looped around her neck, the ends lazily draped over her shoulders. She tugged at her jacket after knocking on the door twice. Moments later a man opened the door, cheerfully greeting Helen. She smiled in response and shook his hand, giving off a warm appearance. They spoke briefly before the man's expression changed, his eyebrows furrowing but his smile staying still. He stepped into the house, leaving Helen by herself. She turned my way, giving me a small hopeful smile before the man came back, holding an object that caused my heart to drop.

I immediately opened the car door and jumped out at the sight of the weapon in his hands, watching Helen step back instantly, raising her hands in surrender. "Stop!" I screamed, causing the man to shift toward me and spontaneously shoot in my direction. I ducked but felt as the bullet grazed my arm, hitting the car door instead. I moved forward and raced for Helen, my heart pounding as I begged him not to shoot.

"You're not taking Joseph! She's a human, just like the rest of us!"

"We're here to protect her!" Helen cried, reaching for me and falling into my arms. The man stared down at us and lowered his gun, sighing.

"Reina didn't mention anyone coming."

Helen raised her hand shakily. "She couldn't. Joseph has murdered two people, and we're here to make sure that she is punished but fairly. Walter was assigned to take care of Joseph, make sure she is kept safe, and kept safe from others," she stuttered, her eyes closed shut as she spoke.

The man dropped his gun, his breathing slowing as his shoulders dropped. "If I were to call Reina, would she know who you all are?"

"Yes. She has been helping us find Joseph," I confirmed. "I am an officer. May I ask why you thought shooting us was necessary?"

Sweat began to form at the top of the man's brows. His hair was thin, and he was overweight. "If anyone else were to find Joseph, they would kill her. I don't care if I go to jail for murder, just as long as Joseph makes it out safely. I'm a good friend of hers."

I sighed, pulling Helen to her feet. "We'd like to take Joseph now unless you'd like to put her in danger."

Charles and Yuuto came from behind the house with Joseph, who was struggling in their grasp. The man turned to face the boys, ready to reach for his gun. "Please call Reina. She will thoroughly explain everything to you. Know that Joseph is in safe hands, we promise."

"Ruth had to die, don't you see? She was hurting everyone!" Joseph exclaimed, kicking her legs outward. The man stood at the door, balling his fists. He watched as Helen stumbled over to the car and pulled out the rope, tying Joseph's hands behind her back.

I stepped forward to the man, nodding to him. "We will take good care of her. Tell anyone that cares about Joseph that she is safe, that she made a mistake and had to go away," I told him.

"Ruth's dead?" the man whispered, no emotion hidden in his words.

I looked down at my hands, the question processing in my head. "Yes, she was murdered two days ago along with her butler."

"A terrible loss, she was a wonderful girl," the man muttered. I bid him farewell, walking to Charles, who awaited my instructions.

"We will return to the cottage courts. There Yuuto will join you and the three of you will promptly return to Lake Tahoe. I will take Joseph somewhere else."

"Promptly, sir. Is there anything else I can do?"

I smiled. "You've done plenty, Charles. Thank you for all your work. I'll meet you at the courts. Helen, are you alright? Were you hurt?"

"Yes, I'm alright, a bit shocked but fine. Are you hurt?" I shook my head and offered her a smile. I shook Charles's hand and looked at the back seat where Helen was sitting, blowing her a kiss before stepping away and getting into Joseph's car, where she sat angrily in the back.

"Going home?" Yuuto asked once I took my seat. I looked at him and smiled widely.

"Not yet. But we're getting close."

"Again?" I asked, watching as Ruth stumbled into my apartment. Her dress was tattered and her cheek was beginning to swell, as well as the top of her lip. I stood up and ran for the first aid kit, hearing Ruth groan as she flopped onto the couch. I swiftly returned, tending to her wounds and attempting to remember if I had any extra clothes for her. "Was it those boys?"

Ruth slowly shook her head, flinching at my touch. "A random person. I asked for it."

"Why?" I asked.

"My brother's dead. He left his fortune to me, said that no one but me can access it. I'm not sure how he did it, but he did. He also left me a marble house in Lake Tahoe apparently, one he was constructing just for me," she began. She sniffled as she spoke, tears forming around her eyes. "I can't believe he's dead."

I reached forward and gently hugged her, placing a kiss at the top of her forehead. "I'm so sorry, Ruth. That's horrid."

"He died of a heart attack supposedly. Doesn't make sense to me, he was in perfect health."

"Do you think someone—"

"No. I hope not," Ruth quickly interrupted, pushing me away. "No one would ever want to hurt my brother, he's

wonderful. He's the only person other than you who was kind to me," she said. Ruth giggled at a memory. "We used to do this thing whenever either of us was upset; we would say something kind to each other, something we meant, to remind each other it's not all bad. I could be having the worst day of my life, but even then my eyes are just as pretty as my mother's."

I finished tending to Ruth's injuries and placed the kit on the coffee table behind me. "It sounds like you and your brother were very close," I said.

"Don't you have a sister?" she asked me.

I nodded, half smiling at the thought of her. "Older, she's a singer."

"A singer? Do you sing?"

"A little."

Ruth gently shifted toward me, her eyes fluttering as she examined me, grinning. "Sing something for me, won't you?"

I knitted my brows at her request, unsure if she was being serious. She watched me intently, waiting, so I began to sing. "This suspense is killing me, I can't stand uncertainty," I began. Ruth's eyes lit up insisting I continue. "Tell me 'no,' I've got to know, whether you want me to stay or go." Ruth shifted in her seat, softly accompanying me. "Love me or leave me, and

*let me be lonely. You won't believe me that I love you only. I'd
rather be lonely, than happy with somebody else."*

I continued to sing, gripping her hand as she stared at
me with awe, fascinated by my voice. She chuckled to herself
once I was done, nodding. "Walter you have a beautiful voice.
You should be a singer too," she advised.

I laughed. "Maybe, later in life. I've always been
engrossed with the opera."

"Then sing opera. I want you to sing, Walter. Share
your voice just like your sister does before it's too late." Her
voice grew quiet, a shaking breath forcing itself into her lungs.

I lifted her hand to my lips and kissed her knuckles,
pushing back her hair as she lay still on the sofa, dried blood on
her neck, bruises growing around her body. I instantly decided
that I never wanted to see her this way ever again, lying on my
sofa with bruises and blood, barely able to move. "You deserve so
much better, Ruth," I said earnestly. She looked up to me,
perplexed by my sudden declaration. "I'll tell you something
nice; even though there are horrors in this world, millions of bad
days and bad people, you always seem to find the good in
everything or spark hope in others, and you never mean to.
Though things are bad now, they will get better, Ruth. There

will come a time when you no longer have to stumble into my home for aid, or need a milkshake after a bad fight. You will change lives."

Ruth studied both my eyes, lifting her hand and placing it on my cheek. My heart fluttered at the touch. "I'll move to Lake Tahoe. I'll live in the house my brother built, and use the money he left behind to help others," she announced.

"That's perfect," I concurred.

"Will you keep on saying nice things to me, Walter?"

"Whenever you need me to."

The sky was growing dark, and my eyelids began to flutter, threatening to close entirely. "Would you like me to drive?" Yuuto asked. I shook my head, insisting I was fine. "If we crash, it's your fault," he muttered, earning a laugh.

"What's Joseph doing?" I asked.

"Waiting," she responded.

Yuuto turned to face her. "For what?"

Joseph smirked. "Your questions. Don't I get a final interrogation?"

Yuuto pressed his right hand on mine, knowing I was beginning to bubble with anger. "How did you do it?" Yuuto asked.

Joseph stayed silent for a moment, causing the sound of her shifting to seem much louder than it really was. "While Eddie and Yuuto went to the wine cellar, I snuck in and took a knife from the kitchen. I went into the library and hid it. Once Walter arrived, I snuck into the library and waited for Ruth to be alone. Then I just . . . walked up to her and stabbed her. I left the knife in her hands, so it'd seem like a suicide, and walked into the dining room looking for Eddie. He would have been my alibi if anything had gone wrong, but he wasn't there. I went back to the ballroom—where I saw Ethel leave the restroom—to check on Ruth, but she was still alive, so I walked back and stabbed her a second time—"

"I need a minute," I grumbled, my stomach beginning to swell. Yuuto caressed my back as he waited for me to compose myself.

After a moment Joseph continued her story. "Once I knew she was dead I ran into the living room and threw the knife out the window." Joseph took a deep breath.

"Then there's Eddie. He didn't deserve to die, but I couldn't let him reveal the murder weapon. While you were off interrogating, I asked Alex to let me use the restroom, where I broke the wine bottle and framed Yuuto. You were looking for broken glass, not a knife. In the morning I heard Ethel talking to Alex, something about breakfast, so I thought we were going to eat. I went downstairs, and by pure chance I caught Eddie holding the knife. I panicked, taking the knife from him and killing him. I thought that if he showed you the knife, you'd realize only Eddie and I were alone in the kitchen at some point, and you'd figure out it was me. I placed the knife in his hands and ran upstairs. No one noticed a thing. I'm surprised I made it this far. I thought I would have been caught before I left the house."

"Are you proud of yourself?" I asked. Joseph pondered my question.

"No. But I did what had to be done. My sister was mistreated, and I couldn't let it go on any longer."

Yuuto knitted his eyebrows together. "Why didn't you kill Abe?"

"There were too many people at the bar, so instead I asked for a drink and left. But I would have killed him if I had the chance. He is just as guilty as Ruth."

My bones ached as I processed Joseph's confession, watching her story play out in my mind. Yuuto and I held each other's hands as we steadied our breathing, guilt overwhelming us both; we could have done much better. I could have solved this much sooner.

"Joseph, I may not know whether or not Ruth went to Heaven or Hell; she may have been awful, but she was also filled to the brim with love and kindness. However, I know for certain where you'll go, and it isn't where the angels dance," Yuuto sneered.

"Right, but I'm sure you will?" Joseph mocked.

Yuuto shook his head, chuckling lightly. "Most certainly not, and I've come to terms with it," he began, turning to glare at Joseph with a deep, hateful stare. "Have you?"

I could have solved the case much sooner, that much is true; I am not as good of a detective as Ruth and the others had believed me to be, that is granted.

But I did what I could. And I can't ever let myself forget it.

An hour or two had passed, and Joseph had gone to sleep. I could tell Yuuto was growing bored of the winding road, and I couldn't help but feel the same.

"What will we do?" I blurted. I immediately regretted it, but knew I couldn't take it back.

Yuuto blinked a couple of times before replying. "About what?"

"About us," I whispered. Yuuto glanced to me before shifting in his seat, nodding.

"You want to talk about us . . . now?" he asked. I asked myself the same thing.

I nervously tapped my foot, staring at the long road ahead. "I want to be with you."

Yuuto's eyes widened, fully moving to face me. "What about Helen?"

"I'll speak to her. We can all talk about this together if you'd like, but the fact of the matter is that I want to be with you."

"We've known each other for two days," Yuuto began. "You've been with Helen for a year. We barely know each other, Walter, and as much as I enjoy your company, I don't want you to throw away what you have with Helen for me. You've just lost someone close to you, and so have I. How are you certain you want to be with me for me, and not because you need someone to care for you?"

I gripped the steering wheel in front of me, processing Yuuto's words. *"Tell him. You don't have to, but you should tell him,"* She whispered, Her words the softest and kindest they'd ever been.

"I had a daughter with Ruby. Her name was Jasmine, and she was an absolute angel," I whispered, feeling my muscles grow stiff as my hands began to vibrate.

"Had?" Yuuto asked quietly.

I nodded once, my jaw growing tense. "She died from the flu at two years old."

Yuuto remained silent, his hands reaching for each other as he processed the information I offered him. He nodded three times as if allowing me to continue.

"Ruby and I suffered greatly. At first she hallucinated, waking up during the night thinking she heard Jasmine babbling. I would spend hours sitting in her room, thinking that doing so would cause her to come back. A close friend of ours came one day and emptied her room, taking her things to his house thinking that it would help us understand she was gone. We spent months floating around the house, barely eating and sleeping. It wasn't until our friend told us we had to keep going that we made small efforts to return to normal life, reminding each other that we had to keep going." I paused and waited for Yuuto to speak, but he kept quiet and waited for me to resume. "I left her months later. I couldn't stand the grief. I couldn't live in that house or see Ruby, or anyone who was close to Jasmine. I ran away from my life, and Ruby let me. Everyone let me. Everyone insisted that it was my way of coping, of moving on."

I glanced toward Yuuto, realizing he was crying. His right hand covered his mouth, preventing him from making a sound. I moved back, breathing harshly and gulping, my chest growing tight while I spoke.

"Why . . . why are you telling me this?" Yuuto choked out.

"Because I run away, Yuuto. I don't ask people to care for me; I leave. But with you, I don't want to run away. I want to stay with you. I don't want to throw away my relationship with Helen, but I don't want to stay. I want to leave as soon as this is all over, but the terrifying part of it all is that I want to leave with you."

"Why me?" he asked in a hushed tone.

I forced a laugh, shrugging. "I'm not sure, but I'm not complaining." I glanced to him once before adding, "I also can't stand simply being friendly with you."

Yuuto laughed, agreeing with me. "We'll have to talk to Helen."

"Of course. And don't worry, she must already suspect something; she's very intelligent."

We sat in silence for some time until Yuuto took my hand, kissing the back of it. "I'm sorry about your daughter."

I flinched at the touch but smiled, looking to him before replying with, "Me too."

Yuuto studied my face before offering a small smile, placing his hand on my cheek and gently kissing my lips, his eyes fluttering shut at the touch. He pulled back and grinned, sitting back in place and falling asleep, his smile still in place.

Chapter Fifteen:

Through Yuuto's Eyes

When we arrived at the cottage courts, Annabelle and Charity greeted us all with a hug. "So you found your killer?" Charity asked, taking a peek toward the second car.

I nodded.

"What now?"

"I'm taking Joseph. Charles, Helen, and Yuuto will stay here today, and tomorrow will return to Lake Tahoe."

"Where are you going?" Annabelle asked, joining the conversation.

I stared at both girls before drifting my sight to my feet, shrugging. "I can't say, but Joseph will be safe. Do take care of those three, won't you?"

Charity grinned. "It's what we're paid to do, Walter. Be careful, won't you?"

I glimpsed to Yuuto and nodded, watching as he laughed at something Brian said. I nodded once more, assuring the girls I would return safely. "Thank you for all you've done, ladies. I will stay in touch."

Before I could head back to Joseph, Charity grabbed my arm, forcing me to face her. "What about Yuuto?"

"I'm taking your advice," I answered, hugging her before hastily walking back to the car and taking Joseph to a safer place.

My name is Yuuto, and it's a surprise to absolutely no one that I may be in love with Walter N. Grover.

I clasped my hands together as Walter waved for the last time, taking Joseph somewhere he refused to share with the rest of us. I admit I felt bitter when he refused to tell me and warned us all that he would never be able to, as if one of us would one day decide to hunt her down and make her pay for her sins.

Then again, the latter did seem likely.

Helen and I shared a room while Charles got his own, which was immensely awkward considering the fact that I was, as I stated before, in love with her husband. I wondered if she felt as uncomfortable as I did.

"What will you do when we return to Tahoe?" Helen effortlessly asked.

I rolled my eyes at the question, already dulled by the conversation. "Go home, sleep as much as possible. By the way, I'm saying this now: I am sleeping on the bed. The couches aren't fun to sleep on, or so Charles told me," I muttered, flopping on the bed. Helen looked behind herself and laughed.

"Do you mind if I sleep on the bed as well?"

I blinked rapidly at her request. "If you don't mind," I mumbled. "What will you do when we return?"

Helen raised her brow at me as if asking about her life was the most questionable thing I could ever do. Oh, how I could prove her wrong. "I'm not certain. With everything that is happening with Germany, I personally don't want to go back, despite my longing for the city. I also know Walter has grown attached to the States, so I doubt we'll be going back anytime soon."

My arms tensed as I chewed on Helen's words, wondering if she meant what I hoped she meant.

Has he grown attached to the States, or me?

"How come you never got to meet Ruth?" I asked, deciding that would be a far more interesting conversation, but just as uncomfortable.

Helen shrugged and opened the now half-empty bag and pulled out a nightdress. "I theorize it's because Walter was in love with her, or because she didn't want to meet me. We invited her to our wedding, but she didn't come. Then she invited me to the party, but Walter lied and said I wasn't. Maybe neither wanted to be with me." Her last words were hushed but loud enough to be heard. Though every fiber in my being insisted I not move and leave her be, I dragged myself out of bed and shuffled over to her, hugging her without saying a word. She slumped into me, something I wasn't expecting.

"Believe me when I tell you that Walter cares about you more than you realize, and Ruth's blessing is not something worth hoping for. You're intelligent and kind. The only opinion that should matter is your own," I advised, stepping away as soon as I could and sitting back on the bed. I looked up and realized Helen was shaking, but there was now a wide smile on her face. She then muttered something about changing and stepped into the restroom.

I looked up at the ceiling and decided now was the best time to think about the terrifying question Annabelle had whispered into my ear before we left the first time.

"Do you love him?"

Of course I do. I *know* I do, but I shouldn't.

Then again, when has that ever stopped me?

I thought about the ride back, how Walter had talked about Jasmine. I wondered if Ruth knew about her, and why he decided to tell me before telling his own wife.

"The fact of the matter is that I want to be with you."

The words ran through my mind endlessly like the crackling at the end of a record, and just like a record, all it would take is a slight adjustment and the sound would end, but I didn't want it to. I never wanted it to.

Good lord, that was dramatic.

The idea of being with Walter was terrifying, considering the things I hadn't realized I didn't know about him, and the many things he didn't know about me. Maybe the reason we both kept secrets is that we feared we would no longer be loved because of our pasts, or we would scare people away. Or maybe that's just me.

No, it isn't.

He runs away, just like I do. After my family banned me from their home I left the country, even though I knew I didn't have to. I had a much better education than most immigrants, I had good friends, and I would have been able to find a job easily and stay somewhere.

But I ran. I ran and I never looked back.

If Walter were there, would I have taken him with me or left him behind?

Or worse, would I have stayed for him?

"What are your thoughts on Walter?" Helen asked as she stepped out of the bathroom, obvious revenge for our previous discussion.

I forcefully laughed and smiled, sitting up on the bed. "I think he's very smart, and I'm glad he finally solved this case. I was dying to get it over with," I said, which was true at some point in time.

"Were you?" She raised an eyebrow.

"Yes." Damn, I answered too quickly.

Helen grinned, leaning against the doorframe of the bathroom. "Are you glad then?"

I stared at her skeptically, unsure of what the correct response would be. The longer I waited to answer, the larger her smile became. "I'm very happy that the killer was caught, and knowing Walter, she'll be punished accordingly."

"But you fear after this Walter will leave you," she spoke with no emotion, which made the question that much harder to answer.

"I'm sure we'll stay in contact."

"But that's not what you want."

I frowned. "Excuse me?"

"Not in the way you want to stay in contact. You want to see him as much as you have these past two day, but you fear that once the case is over your relationship will be restricted to phone calls and meetings once or twice a year."

I raised an eyebrow and crossed my arms, impressed at her confidence. Not at all the Helen Walter had described while we waited in the living room. "You are correct," I admitted.

Helen nodded, strolling over to the bed and sitting next to me. "Do you love him?" she whispered into my ear.

I'd truly appreciate it if people stopped questioning me about it, actually.

"Not at all, I only admire his company."

"That's a pity, because he loves you." She sighed.

My eyes widened as my hands raised to my chest, shifting to face her. "Did he say something?" I whispered, immediately embarrassed by my surrender.

Helen smiled with saddened eyes. My hands fell once I remembered who exactly I was speaking to. "His eyes brighten at the sight of you, and he doesn't even realize it. They did the same at the thought of Ruth. You both also get along very well, and you seem to understand him better than I do. In two days you managed to gain the trust I desperately wanted for a very long time."

"I'm sorry," I said.

Helen shrugged and dropped her smile. "I know he loved me once, long ago. But I messed up. I pretended to be someone I wasn't in order to impress him, to seem worthy of his love, and that's when I lost him. The moment I lost myself, I lost him as well." I wrapped my arms around her, feeling her tense but gradually indulge in my embrace. "I only want him to be happy, and every effort I make to help him fails miserably. It's your turn now, to help him. Don't mess it up as I did."

I waited in silence before replying, tightening my hold on her. "We can both help him. This is your second chance, Helen, don't you see? He needs us, more than you realize. He will trust you because you are loving and intelligent and you have waited long enough for him. We can help him together."

Helen pulled away and studied my eyes, her lip quivering. "Could we?"

I kissed her forehead and smiled, drawing her into a hug. "We certainly can."

Couldn't we?

I wasn't able to return to Lake Tahoe until two months later.

I walked up to Reina's door and knocked twice, then stepped away and admired the forest, taking in the smell of nature and the sound of the river not too far from the home.

"Walter? It can't be you," were the first words I heard once the door opened. I turned around and smiled, immediately embraced by Reina. "How is my sister?"

I hugged her back, allowing myself to indulge in her kindness. "She is well. She has been given a new identity. Her name is now Anastasia Becker. You will be the only person other than me who will know of her whereabouts."

"May I visit her?"

"Not at the moment, but hopefully there will come a day soon enough when you will," I said.

"Where is she?"

"Europe," was all I said. "When I am able to, I will give you more information."

Reina took a step back and grinned. Her eyes brimmed with tears. "Europe? How?"

"Ruth's name can do a lot more than one realizes; she and her family have many resources, and I was able to use them due to Ruth's constant talk about me. Upon her death, she decided to leave her small fortune to me, which opened many doors for me. Know I went to great lengths to make sure your sister will be safe, and everything will be fine. I promise you."

Reina engulfed me in another hug. She held onto me tighter as she sobbed uncontrollably onto my shoulder. "You didn't have to do this for her, truly."

I patted her back and nodded, pushing her hair away from my face. "You know, I thought about that, but then I figured, if I can pull this off, then why shouldn't I?" I waited for her crying to grow soft before continuing, "However, know Anastasia is also paying for her crimes accordingly."

Reina bobbed her head and sniffled, lifting her left hand to her nose. "Yes, of course." She paused. "Anastasia, what a beautiful name."

"She chose it. It's Russian. It means rebirth."

Reina smiled. "I love it. Have you spoken to Helen or Yuuto?"

Yuuto. The mention of his name did not fail to bring a smile to my face. "Not yet. Where are they?"

"I believe they're both staying with Ethel. Would you like the address?"

"Yes please," I answered, then left as soon as I could.

I arrived at Ethel's home an hour after meeting Reina, and I could feel my heartbeat grow stronger as I slammed the car door shut. I looked over my reflection, pushing strands of hair into place and finally shuffling up the driveway, excitement running along my veins.

I hesitated before knocking on the door. *Two months.*

The door creaked open to reveal a woman with brown hair that I had wrongly accused of murder two months ago. Her brown hair was neatly pulled back into a bun. "Heavens," she breathed out, once she fully recognized me.

"Are they here?"

"You're back," she ignored my question.

"Are they here?" I asked again.

Ethel reached out and hugged me, laughing. "You baboon, won't you say hello first? It's been months since any of us saw you."

I chuckled and hugged her back. "I'm terribly sorry. I just want to see them as soon as I can. How have you been?"

"As well as one can be. Liza sends her regards." She studied my face before giggling, nodding approvingly of me. "You look so different; your hair's a bit longer and you've got peach fuzz. Where did you go?"

"I'm afraid I can't reveal that. But Joseph is in good hands."

Ethel invited me into her house, which looked similar to Reina's. However it was smaller, her living room, dining room, and kitchen together in one large room. "Yuuto! Helen! Could you come down?" she called out, then turned to me. "Helen didn't have a place to stay, so she's been living with me, and Yuuto comes by so often he practically lives here now. They've become incredibly good friends," she informed me. I raised my eyebrows and began to phrase a question before I was interrupted by Yuuto's complaining as he made his way downstairs.

"Really, Ethel, there's no need to shout—" Yuuto abruptly stopped speaking once he saw me.

His hair was pushed back and he wore a black vest that covered a white shirt with bishop sleeves. A blue scarf was wrapped around his neck and his trousers were a dark blue. His eyes were wide, but there were visible bags beneath them, and his hands twitched slightly as he stared at me with surprise.

"Hello, Yuuto," I choked out, unable to say anything else. *I was gone for two months doing a good thing, but all I could think about was running back to you,* I wanted to admit, but I couldn't form any words, dumbfounded by the gorgeous sight before me.

"Yuuto, what did Ethel need?" Helen asked, stepping into the room shortly after Yuuto and gasping immediately. Her hair dripped over her shoulders, and she wore a long green gown with cuffed sleeves.

Both stared intently at me, both unsure of what to do. I decided to step closer, but the action surprised the duo, so I moved back.

"Two months," Helen hissed, though she didn't sound upset. "Was two months as soon as you could come back?" Her voice was cracking by the end of her sentence.

"I worked as quickly as I could," I argued. "I didn't mean to take so long—"

"Shut up," Yuuto exclaimed, reaching a hand out toward Helen. She took it with no hesitation. "Shut up, I need to think," he said.

"About what?" I asked.

"What to do," he replied, as if it were the most obvious thing in the world.

"About?" I questioned, confused.

Yuuto nodded to himself before letting go of Helen's hand and strutting across the room, gently placing a hand on my cheek and grabbing me by my neck before pulling me into a deep kiss.

I jumped before giving into the kiss, wrapping my arms around his shoulders as I returned the passion, holding him as tightly as I could. It wasn't until I pulled back to breathe that I noticed he was crying. "You're a damn fool, Walter. I thought you were never coming back." He sighed, immediately kissing me again.

"I was a damn fool to leave you in the first place," I said huskily, moving my lips to the nape of his neck and laughing, feeling Yuuto kiss my hair and giggle to himself.

After what felt like years of laughter and kisses, Ethel moved forward and pulled Yuuto back, laughing herself. "Calm down, boys, don't get too excited." I grinned as I examined Yuuto, realizing his once neat, pushed back hair was in ruins.

"Will I get a similar greeting?" Helen joked from the doorway. My heart dropped, and I raced to think of an excuse until she raised her hand and shook her head. "Walter, it's okay, don't worry," she quickly assured me, but the feeling in my stomach remained.

"Helen—"

"Yuuto and I have become wonderful friends since you've been gone, and I haven't met anyone who cares about you as much as he does. The amount of times I had to talk him out of setting up his own search party for you is too many to keep track of, and I know you feel the same way about him. If you want to leave me I completely understand—"

Before she could finish her sentence I ran over and drew her into a hug, resulting in her sudden silence. She gradually lifted her arms and hugged me back, her breath quivering as she did so.

"I missed you," I whispered into her ear, kissing her cheek.

Helen grinned and dug her chin into my shoulder. "I missed you too."

"You'll have to see Alex after. She went insane when she found out you went on your own with Joseph," Ethel began.

"Alex assisted me throughout my trip. She was the only one I could call while I was away; however, I gave her strict orders not to mention it to any of you. Otherwise you could all have been put in danger," I admitted. Ethel gawked while Helen and Yuuto shook their heads, looking over at each other with the same unsurprised expression.

"You should still tell her you're back," a voice piped up from behind me, "so she knows she gave all the right instructions and didn't end up killing you."

I turned around and smiled at Alex, chuckling before hugging her. "Why are you here?" I asked.

"Reina phoned me, told me you were back in town and you'd be here. How'd it go?"

I drew back and scanned Alex, admiring her long, curled hair and her floral dress. "Joseph is under a new identity and well protected. She is paying for her crimes, and it's safe to say none of us will ever see her again."

"Except for you," Helen chimed in.

"And Reina," I added. Alex nodded and shook my hand, walking past me and standing next to Ethel, who was leaning against a counter.

The group made their way into the living room, all of them taking a seat around each other, waiting to tell me about what had happened in the past two months. No doubt they would speak of the war, but we all knew there were more pressing subjects that had to be discussed. I looked closely at all of the people, noting their calm and happy faces; all were at peace and ready to move on or possibly forget.

I pressed my lips together and took it all in. *"They're all so peculiar, aren't they? An explorer with a fear of everything, a woman with a second personality, a writer with a wish to be an average housewife, and a former drug dealer with a drinking problem,"* She noticed from beside me. "Not any more peculiar than we are, right, Ruby?" I replied. I turned to look at Her.

But she was gone.

Epilogue

"Chin up, angel. I need to see what I'm doing," I spoke, tying the blue scarf around the toddler's neck. "We want you to look your best for the party, don't we?"

The little girl bobbed her head up and down in excitement. "Papa knows I wear his scarf?"

I shook my head and grinned. "Not yet, but we'll show him now." The girl opened and closed her hands, signaling she wanted to be picked up. I lifted her and placed her before the mirror, allowing her to admire her blue jumper and her curled brown hair. She patted the scarf around her neck and beamed, approving of her look. With the child still in my arms, I stepped out of the room and walked down the stairs, grinning as Yuuto and Charles lifted a table and placed it in the center of the ballroom. Yuuto stepped back to wipe the sweat from his brow and then noticed us come in.

"Ruby, my angel, look at you! You look lovely!" he exclaimed, causing the toddler to jump in my arms with glee.

"Papa!" she screamed, reaching out for Yuuto. He grabbed her hands and kissed her fingers before looking up and kissing me.

"She's wearing my scarf," he noticed. I nodded.

"It was her idea," I told him, to which Ruby nodded happily.

Yuuto laughed and stroked the scarf before stepping back. "Have you shown Ma how beautiful you look, my dear?"

"Daddy said to show you now!" Ruby announced.

Yuuto kissed her forehead. "Of course he did. Come, let's show Ma. She's taking care of Samuel," he said, taking Ruby from my arms.

"Alex said she'd be arriving early. Ironic, isn't it? Ethel is coming, so is Reina and the Mallorys. Also Ruby and Thomas will be late," Yuuto told me, walking out of the ballroom. I waved to Charles before leaving with Yuuto and Ruby.

"Ruby and Thomas?" I asked, surprised.

Yuuto nodded. "I found Ruby's number while I was boxing up Ruth's notes. Thought I'd give her a call and invite her to the party. She seems lovely, by the way. She can't wait to meet our Ruby."

"Does she know about—"

"She knows nothing. I told her I know you, we're throwing a party, and you have a baby. I thought that might convince her to come. Now, if you're angry with me you can yell about it later, but—"

I grabbed Yuuto's chin and spun him, kissing him gently. "I'm not angry. Thank you for inviting her." Yuuto blushed in response.

We made our way out into the entrance and up the stairs, walking to the back and knocking on Helen's door. She muttered, "Come in," allowing us to enter. I stepped in and grinned at the sight of Helen. She was happily breastfeeding Samuel, who gurgled in response to the sudden disturbance. "How may I help you lads?" she asked, then noticed Ruby tugging at her scarf. Helen gasped and asked Yuuto to come closer, taking the scarf into one of her hands. "Oh, Ruby, you look beautiful my love!" she whispered excitedly, not wanting to bother the baby in her arms. Ruby lifted her chin proudly in order for Helen to get a better look, earning a laugh from the woman. "Now tell your fathers to fix themselves so they look just as lovely as you do," she teased.

"We're already dressed," I argued.

Helen raised an eyebrow. "You are absolutely not wearing that, either of you. Why don't you wear the suits our little Ruby got for you two?"

Yuuto knit his brows in confusion. "Suits?"

The room went quiet for a minute. "I'm terribly sorry, I forgot to tell you. Christmas two years ago we all got you presents. We wanted to give them to you, but the soldiers at the internment camp said no one was allowed to visit," Helen whispered. Yuuto nodded once, his hand twitching in response.

"I see. Well, hopefully, it fits. I did lose a drastic amount of weight," he whispered, placing Ruby next to Helen before stepping out of the room. I followed behind him.

"Yuuto—"

Yuuto gripped his hands together before facing me, his lip quivering. "I missed so much while I was at the camp. I missed Samuel's birth, our daughter's first words, her first birthday—"

I reached out for his arm and pulled him close, stroking the scar on his arm that reminded us all of the terrible injustice he had suffered for three years. "You would have been killed if you didn't go, Yuuto. You did what was right. There was nothing any of us could have done to prevent what was," I began. "But the war is finally over, and you're finally home. You may have missed out on three years' worth of events, but you will have years to come to make up for it. We need to keep going, remember?" I softly kissed Yuuto's lips before intertwining his hands with mine.

"We need to keep going," Yuuto whispered in response, squeezing my hand and following me upstairs.

The room was overcome with excitement, old friends laughing and catching up on each other's lives. I walked over to Annabelle and Charity, who were both speaking to Helen. "The man of the hour! How have you been?" Charity exclaimed, moving forward and shaking my hand.

"Splendid, and how are you both?"

"Couldn't be better. However, never mind us, what about you? You have a child!" Charity said excitedly.

I looked to Helen, who only smiled in return. "Her name is Ruby; she's three. Yuuto and I wanted to have a child, so Helen volunteered to help us and gave birth to Ruby. We couldn't be happier," I told them.

"Helen was telling us about Samuel. Did you and Helen have him as well?" Annabelle asked.

I shook my head. "No, Helen had Samuel with another man so the baby would be all hers. Did she tell you about her novel?"

"She did! Helen, I cannot wait to read it. I'm sure it'll be amazin," Charity answered.

We spoke a bit longer about Helen's book and the children until I noticed the ballroom doors open.

I immediately left the group and began walking toward the newcomers, my heart racing at the sight. I walked past Yuuto, who was playing with our daughter; Alex, who was laughing at one of Ethel's jokes; and Reina, who was having a loving conversation with Brian Mallory.

The music faded away as my attention focused on the figure ahead.

"Walter?" Ruby whispered. I could have broken down sobbing at that very moment.

"Ruby," I whispered in disbelief.

She stared at me before looking around the ballroom, smiling softly as Thomas entered the room behind her. He had a beard now.

"Did Ruth leave this place behind for you?" Ruby asked. I nodded, unable to form a sentence. "I figured. You were both very close. I'm terribly sorry about your loss. It's been four years now, hasn't it?"

I nodded again.

Ruby's eyes wandered and fell upon Yuuto, smiling at the giggling toddler. "I assume that's your daughter, Ruby. A magnificent name if I may say so myself," she joked.

"You're okay," I choked out.

Ruby nodded, taking Thomas's hand in hers. "I told you I would be."

I stared at their hands, grinning widely. I noticed a
ring on Ruby's finger. "Congratulations," I said. Ruby
giggled.

"Thank you. Now, who is the new Mrs. Grover?"

I looked to Yuuto and pointed to him. "Mr. Grover,
actually. That's Yuuto. You spoke to him on the phone.
He's my husband. Well, at least he would be if we could
get married. Helen over there is Ruby's mother, but Ruby
belongs to Yuuto and me. She has a baby, Samuel. He was
born a few months ago." I beamed with pride as I looked
at all of them.

"Look at you, Walter. My wonderful detective,
now with a beautiful home and an entire family. I'm
sovery proud of you," she stated, moving closer and
cupping my chin. "We kept going, and we made it."

I felt tears begin to stream down my cheeks as I
nodded, drawing Ruby into a hug. We held each other
tightly, and it wasn't until Yuuto patted my back that I
realized it was time. Alex stopped the music and everyone
sat down, leaving Yuuto, Helen, and I standing in the
center of the room. "On this day six years ago, two of our
beloved friends, Ruth Chapman and Edward Lee Alton,

died a terrible death. It wasn't until three days later that their killer was caught and brought to justice," I began. "As horrible as these losses were, they would not want us to mourn, but to carry on and live our lives happily, never looking back. Today we commemorate the lives of Eddie and Ruth, but we also celebrate new beginnings; may it be with old friends or new, new aspirations or ideas, it does not matter. Just as long as we continue to move forward. Cheers!"

The group raised their glasses and cheered, chatting with the people around them. Yuuto stepped in front of me and wrapped his arms around my waist, pulling me into a kiss. I gave in happily, taking in his taste and his warmth.

Long ago I thought the only true love in my life would be Ruth, but she only wanted to impress me, and I only wanted to fix her, and I see now we never truly loved each other, only burdened one another. As time went on her heart grew sicker, and mine grew weaker, to the point where obsession was disguised as affection and the only thing worth living for was a woman who ran from her problems by solving others. At some point in time, I could have said with complete confidence that she was an angel sent from the heavens, but she was just as flawed as the rest of us, and as human as me.

I used to believe that Ruth was the happiest person I knew, but that was not at all the case. She lived a difficult life, one which did not excuse her later behavior, but still, she did not deserve.

Ruth was many things to many people: a liar, a savior, a saint, or a manipulator. To me, she was all. But she was also my best friend, and a girl who so desperately wanted to change the world in hopes it would change her.

If I had known the day after Ruth's death that the man who had tucked me into bed would become the love of my life, that the bed I had slept in would become mine, and the people who roamed throughout the house would become my greatest companions,

I would have never gone back to sleep.

Acknowledgements

This was never meant to become a novel, or anything more than two chapters, but here we are now.

Huge thanks to my mother, obviously, because if it weren't for her you wouldn't be able to read this. I wrote this but she did practically everything else. Also, I don't think anyone will be able to put up with me the way she has. She deserves the world.

Thank you to my editors for the amazing feedback and not going easy on me just because I'm a teenager.

Of course, thanks to Hannah, Maddie, and Nat for somehow having the patience to read this story as it was being written and allowing me to watch this story unfold through the eyes of someone who had absolutely no idea how it was going to end.

Huge thanks to the United Staters of course; they don't have to be as supportive as they are, but they are anyways.

I'd also like to thank my teachers. Not only for their support, but because I spent many of their classes writing this book instead of taking notes, and I'm almost positive the majority were aware but let me get away with it (I promise that they were doing their jobs, I just wasn't). They also showed actual interest in my writing even though they didn't have to, and it means the world to me.

There are some teachers I'd especially like to thank. Mrs. Brochu for helping with the historical aspect of this book, Mrs. DaSilva for letting me write during class as long as I kept up with work, Mrs. Pickford for her enthusiasm, and Mrs. Meystre and Mrs. Watson for having faith in me and offering constant support even after I left the middle school.

Thanks to my sister, who's practically my other half and chose to sit through my many hour long rants about this book; I have no idea how I'll make it up to her but I'm seriously thankful she listened even though she didn't understand. Not only that, but she has to deal with me almost all the time and I know how hard that can be sometimes. She also deserves the world.

Thanks to my dad, who's always challenging me and pushing me out of my comfort zone. I hope you read this before the movie. Te quiero.

Gracias a mi familia en México, por que aun que no estemos juntos siempre pienso en ustedes, y agradezco su apoyo incondicional en todos mis sueños, mis locuras y mis caprichos.

And finally, thanks to You.

Made in the USA
Middletown, DE
06 February 2020